# THE GROUSE CONSPIRACY

Martyn Chapman

*Dedications*

*\* To memories, moments, and friendships.*

*\* To Nick and his little blue car.*

*With thanks to:*

*\* Amazon and the publishing professionals who have guided and helped me through the writing process.*

*With very special thanks to:*

*\* Korčula – the delightful locals and gracious visitors that make the hot summer months so special. See you again soon.*

# CONTENTS

# CHAPTER ONE

Her arrival took me by surprise. I was sitting at one of the hotel's sleek white tables, my imagination drifting idly across the infinity pool to savour the magnificent blue cove beyond. Moments. They come, they scar, they tumble, dropping nonchalantly into our lives like snowflakes — catch them on your tongue. Moments that are random, unpredictable, yet generous. Something will always remain. The imprint of an insect's tiny wing or a fragment of time that will help construct a defining memory, help to form a wonderful relationship. And one of these moments happened on the stunning island of Korčula. A dazzling moment that would stay with me forever.

"This is fucking gross," Olivia said, obstinately kicking a chair away from the table. "How ridiculous! You could have at least sat inside the breakfast area this morning."

I reluctantly abandoned the view of the bay and pushed my spoon into a congealed bowl of muesli. "I assume you're referring to the light gust."

"It's more like a hurricane." She waved a lazy finger towards a turquoise napkin that was fluttering gently in the wind. "*See!* Just ridiculous."

"Look, let's be absolutely clear about this," I said grudgingly. "I did not try to murder your mother."

She stared at me indignantly, and then her eyes flickered as if disbelieving my words, disbelieving that she had been betrayed.

"I heard what you said this morning," I continued, "and yes, I can understand that you might have been upset . . ."

"*Might.*"

"Okay, you were upset. But it's not my fault that your mother is ill."

"You chose the restaurant."

"That has nothing to do with it, and I'd happily go back there. I'm not sick. *Are you sick?*"

"How should I know?" She let her pink rucksack tumble heavily onto the grey tiles of the terrace and swung her body elegantly towards the breakfast area of the hotel. "I'm not a doctor."

"No," I mumbled as I watched her leave. "You're a pain in the behind."

Olivia wasn't my daughter.

I did not have children. I had never wanted any children, and the eight months that I'd spent warily circling Olivia's bolshie and venomous moods had strongly reinforced this. But she was no longer a child. Olivia was just a few weeks away from her eighteenth birthday. Modern society is obsessed with a blame culture, and some experts would attribute Olivia's stroppy and selfish behaviour to her parents' divorce, nurture or puberty. But I put it down to genes, and nature had been very cruel to Olivia — she had inherited her father's genes. I had never heard of Francis Charles Lawler until I was introduced to his delightful ex-wife at the village Social Club. Our innocuous club would become a welcome place of refuge for Juliet, as she knew that it was the one building in the village that Francis would never enter. He was a snob. The President of the local golf club, although there was certainly no animosity between the two societies, and it was his golfing buddies who were now queuing up to tell me what an obnoxious and pompous man he was. This had led to many uneasy questions about why Juliet had married such a man, although she was adamant that it was down to youth, naivety, and the fact that he had changed. But the latter seemed unlikely to me, because even at a young age, Olivia was already showing his ugly traits. *Changed from what?* I had often pondered.

I wanted to see if Olivia would return to the table before I went back to the breakfast buffet. This was our third morning at the hotel, and I'd noticed that she was notoriously slow and fastidious with her food choices. I had no complaints and thought that the breakfast buffet was extensive and inviting, and partly to avoid the cost of lunch, I usually made three or four enthusiastic visits. Yet, from the childish sounds and facial expressions Olivia had made, it was clear that my indulgence irritated her. On the second morning, I had reluctantly decided that it was not worth the aggravation to pick up a bundle of tomato sauce sachets. But time was short today, and I knew I would have to restrict myself to just a couple of sausages, a fried egg, and a chunk of cheese. Maybe a large chunk of cheese.

Olivia made her graceful return to the terrace, accentuating a little shiver to make her point about the breeze. Her petulance was beginning to amuse me, because I guessed that the air temperature had already reached the mid-twenties. Yes, perhaps the strength of the wind was increasing, although it certainly wasn't a hurricane. After a brief inspection of the chair, she placed a bowl of yoghurt and a glass of pineapple juice on the table.

"Just to be perfectly clear about this," she said, "I'm only doing this for her."

"You mean you've decided to go on the trip to appease your mother?"

"Of course," she snarled, as if this noble gesture merited some special recognition.

Juliet had originally pre-booked the excursion for the two of us, because Olivia was adamant that she wouldn't want to come along. Apparently, another day sitting by the swimming pool was far more appealing than a *silly boat trip*. At the time I had struggled to stifle my glee. After the shock of discovering that Olivia was going to join us for a week in Croatia, this had been the only encouraging part of the holiday. Wisely, I had kept a dignified silence throughout the preparations. My relationship with Juliet was too fresh to make any objections, and after eight years of living on my own, any opportunity to travel abroad was welcome.

I left Olivia to scrutinise a large piece of fruit in her yoghurt, wondering if this rogue item would be discreetly removed and placed on top of the whitewashed wall that demurely circled the terrace. Two mornings earlier, a similar piece of fruit had been merrily described as a 'gift for the sweet little birds'. She hadn't been amused when I had cheekily suggested that the sweet little birds might choke on it. Not that this was a surprise. Olivia did not appear to indulge in any form of humour.

On my way to the buffet, I was forced to avoid a collision with another guest who was restlessly pacing up and down with a mobile phone thrust to the side of his ear. It appeared to be his morning ritual. He even wore the same baggy mauve T-shirt and matching shorts. The phone call would usually end with a loud grunt, and then he'd stomp across the terrace to join a young woman and toddler. Curiously, despite speaking in English to his companions, he always used a different language whilst on the phone. This left me to speculate if he was talking to a work colleague, his wife, or another child.

It had been five past two in the morning when I realised that Juliet had a serious problem. I was awoken from a deep slumber by noises that resembled nothing that I had ever heard from a woman before. My dreams had conjured up the image of a meercat with its tail stuck inside the door of the minibar. It was the first time in our relationship that I had heard Juliet being sick, and I soon discovered that she was the sort of person who liked to face her demons alone. A flapping hand waved me away, and the bathroom door was kicked closed by her bare foot. It would be another four hours before we spoke.

Juliet had suffered a wretched night, and there was no way that she could face getting on a boat or risk sampling any wine. She just wanted to drink plenty of water and try and get some sleep. But as the cost of the trip could not be reimbursed, she wanted me to take her delightful daughter instead. Trying desperately to mask the panic in my face, I had made a flimsy argument of why I should go solo. 'Olivia can stay and look after you,' my voice had croaked in a similar manner to her own. Yet this suggestion had made Juliet even more resolute, and at half past seven in the morning, she had insisted on dragging her weary bones to the room next door. For nearly ten minutes I had crossed my fingers, legs, toes, kidneys, listening to the muffled sound of voices and hoping that Olivia would put up a better fight than my own. But the stupid girl had failed, and now a long and very miserable day lay ahead.

# CHAPTER TWO

I had promised Juliet that we would not disturb her. So, after finishing our breakfast, I gingerly suggested to Olivia that we should head to the jetty where the boat was due to collect us. Her reaction was predictable. She sighed heavily, lobbed her head sideways to snatch a glance of her beloved infinity pool, and then reluctantly followed me down the stone steps towards the sea.

It had been three years since I had run my last half marathon, but now the memories of that sunny morning in York had returned, and it was difficult to stifle the urge to break into a jog. *No, a sprint.* I already felt chained to Olivia and desperately wanted to escape her. My head was a mush of numbness and anxiety, like the initial shock of feeling your feet slip on an icy surface. She was a few paces behind me, although I could sense that each foot was planted with malice and resentment. Familiar voices exploded inside my head. *What am I doing here? Why did I ever have to meet her mother? Why didn't Olivia get sick, too? Wasn't I happy living the bachelor lifestyle?*

But the truth was that I was very fond of Juliet, and this situation had nothing to do with our relationship. She had a daughter, and unfortunately, this petulant and annoying teenager was a replica of her despicable father.

I realised that even Olivia's sluggish movements had now ground to a halt.

"What's wrong?" I asked, hoping that she was having second thoughts.

"The hotel water taxi," she muttered, her lips continuing to quiver as they whispered two extra words — "you idiot."

"No. The water taxi doesn't take us to where we need to go."

"What do you mean?"

"I mean, we have to walk around the bay."

"That's ridiculous."

"Why?" I said, trying to taper my impatience. "You successfully made the same trip on foot last night."

"Yes, but I'd had a drink."

"So the alcohol propels you along, does it?"

"Of course. *And it wasn't during the heat of the day.*"

She had the annoying habit of scrunching her nose up when she thought that she was being clever. Even her mother had commented on it.

"Perhaps it's easier without alcohol in the system," I said. "Anyway, the breeze should keep us cool."

"Monsoon! There is no way that we can go swimming in this!"

Despite her negativity and the frustrating manner in which she twisted every statement to suit her own selfish agenda, I was also getting a little concerned about the weather. The sky was a gorgeous deep blue, yet it had a nasty cough, and there was a real venom on the surface of the sea. "Things can change."

"Yes, in a bad way."

To my surprise, after some reluctant forward momentum in Olivia's legs, she did continue to walk down the path. Perhaps she had decided that I was right about the hotel water taxi, or by agreeing to this foolish act, she would get some concession in return. This was probably a trait that belonged to her father and was the reason why he seemingly made so much money. His new blonde girlfriend certainly dressed well, although the amount of cosmetic surgery she had endured made it impossible to predict her age. Olivia rarely mentioned the woman, but she had dropped hints that she was only in her early thirties. Juliet was adamant that she was more like forty-four.

For most tourists, it was a lovely ten-minute walk around the inlet. Set amongst the tall pines, there was a winding concrete path on the rim of the shoreline which stretched from the hotel grounds to the end of the bay. Small multi-coloured boats pitched and struggled against their moorings, and on the opposite side, pretty houses reclined against the rock face and gorged the fruit of the sea.

We passed the restaurant where we had eaten on the previous evening. I could see our simple blue table. It was on the paved terrace just a few feet above the water, and hidden beneath the rail, there was a row of submerged lights that had drawn the crabs out from the darkness. These quirky underwater lights had justified my choice of the restaurant. They were the lights that had briefly made Olivia laugh and excitedly point out yet another of our curious visitors. It had felt like the best evening of the holiday so far, and I had gazed at the brooding shadows of the boats, eagerly looking forward to the excursion the next morning. It seemed so long ago now after Juliet's horrendous night's sleep.

Whatever had upset her stomach, I doubted it had anything to do with the restaurant. I hadn't joined the girls for lunch at the beach café, choosing to meander along the forest path with a large bottle of water. Later, Juliet had mentioned something about a clumsy waitress and an interesting tuna salad. But as Olivia had kindly pointed out to me: *I was not a doctor.*

Olivia was clearly surprised when I took a sharp right turn instead of heading on down the road towards Korčula's Old Town. It was a narrow and fenced passage that led to the entrance of an abandoned hotel, and I sensed her annoyance and anxiety as she wearily avoided clumps of old concrete and pieces of metal wire. I could not summon the energy to explain where I was going, although it dawned on me that she was having to place some trust in my judgement. Something that she was not used to doing. During my visits to her mother's house, we had developed an effective plan of avoidance. It was like mastering a bizarre shuffling dance that used craned necks and tilted heads to avoid all eye contact. Fortunately, she would usually take the initiative by staying in her bedroom, but if she did happen to be in the living room, I would never enter without Juliet. I wasn't aware that she had bothered to find out anything about me, and Juliet had never mentioned such a conversation. Perhaps Olivia hoped that I would disappear like the last irritating boyfriend, and then her mother would move on with her life.

"There's a jetty somewhere around here," I reluctantly broke the silence, "and this route should be the quickest way to reach it."

She didn't answer me, and all I could think was that I was right. *She really did want me to disappear.*

The desolation of the building surprised and unsettled me. Windows were either cracked or boarded up, and a gap in a heavy and forlorn curtain revealed the stacked chairs of a once bustling dining room. It seemed incredulous that a hotel on such a beautiful island could end up like this. *What happened to the laughter and the happy holiday memories? Where does it all go?* The hotel's abandonment felt like a metaphor for the bachelor lifestyle that I had left behind.

"Nearly there," I mumbled, relieved to see that a corridor of stone steps would lead us down to a concrete jetty. "We're nearly there."

"This can't be it," she said grouchily.

"I'm pretty sure that it is. It's only likely to be a small boat."

"What? Are you kidding? Who would be stupid enough to set sail in this hurricane? If it's a small boat, we'll drown!"

I stared out to sea and saw a tussle of swirling currents and colours that resembled a deranged artist's palate. "Let's see who else has turned up," I suggested feebly.

A deserted seafront answered my question and all I could think of doing was to fumble inside my pocket for my mobile phone.

"Dear God, and how is that dinosaur going to help us?"

I ignored her and fumbled for the 'on' key. *This dinosaur receives bloody text messages.*

"And who organised this ridiculous excursion?" Olivia demanded. Her assertive tone gave the impression of a respected businesswoman who ran a multimillion-pound company.

"Unfortunately, it was booked through your mother's email address and I'm just wondering if there have been any updates."

She sighed heavily. "My poor mother is ill in bed."

I waited for the whispered 'idiot' but this time it didn't pop out of her mouth.

"Yes," I agreed, "but with her phone on, it would appear. The organiser has sent a message." With Olivia's eyes boring into me, I read Juliet's text. "Okay, that's good. Someone has been in touch to let us know that the start of the trip has been delayed for an hour. A decision will be made at ten o'clock."

"And what is *good* about that news?"

I raised my arms and gestured to the jetty. "Because now we know why there is no one else here."

"I'm not walking back and forth to the hotel all morning. I'm busy."

I considered the first part of her objection for a moment. The second statement was too ridiculous to bother with. "You don't have to. We can walk into the Old Town and wait there."

"Pointless. It would be obvious to a blind cat that we can't sail today."

"Sunbathing won't be much fun either, and didn't you say last night that you wanted some pretty 'blue sky' photographs to send to your father? It might be windy, but there are very few clouds." This reference to 'Daddy' appeared to be the deciding factor, and instead of retracing her steps, she moved along the promenade in the direction of the old boathouse.

\*\*\*

By the time I had summoned enough desire to catch her up, Olivia had reached an area of the sea that had been roped off. Something had concerned or frustrated her, and I assumed that it was either linked to the weather or food poisoning. Perhaps she had discovered a small brown bottle with the word 'cyanide' written on the label. "Is this some sort of weird aquarium?" she asked sourly, her fingers tugging a strand of blonde hair from the strap of her rucksack.

"What?" I mumbled.

"This . . . weird aquarium place."

"Oh, well I suppose it depends on your opinion of people who play water polo," I answered jadedly, staring at the neat rectangular playing area. "It looks so unappealing that I think they must be quite weird."

"Not as strange as snooker players."

I was taken aback by her comment, but also felt flattered that she knew a little bit about my interests. "Or golfers."

"It doesn't compare," she snapped back at me. "Golf is a proper sport."

"No, I've had this accusation thrown at me before. They are quite similar if you think about it. We use a green baize to play on, and our objective is to get a ball into a little round hole. Doesn't that sound familiar?"

"You don't have nature, though. My Daddy sees hawks and deer during his rounds of golf."

"You're right there. And we don't have deer poo, soggy leaves, mud or sunstroke."

She walked a few paces away from me and stopped. "What about the horrible smoke?"

"Smoke? What smoke?"

"Those disgusting old man who smoke cigarettes all day."

"No one smokes inside the club — that's illegal. Anyway, golf clubs have smokers, too."

"Maybe, but the Social Club is a hovel."

Despite her offensive comments about my fellow Social Club members and friends, I was intrigued that she had mentioned smokers. I'd heard a rumour that her father had protested to the Local Council about the 'scruffy and vulgar' men who stand in the street with stumpy cigarettes in their hands. But the building was wedged between two shops, and we didn't have anywhere to stand at the rear of the property. Besides, George, Robbo, and Sinclair were some of the most generous and jovial members of our little club.

"I'll recommend that it's turned into a bingo hall when I return," I said.

We climbed up to the main road and wandered past the snake

of bars and restaurants that nestled on the outskirts of the Old Town. At night, this was a popular stopping place for teenagers and young couples with pushchairs. Juliet had suggested that we try one of these restaurants later in the week, which had immediately received my approval. The prices were cheaper than the wine bars and candlelit bistros that were situated amongst the towering ancient walls, the places that were favoured by the wealthy yacht owners and folk who didn't play bingo.

After turning right by the bus station, we had our first view of their luxurious boats. They bobbed zealously against their moorings, their hypnotic motion reminding me of a dog bounding after a stick. And sitting majestically beyond the yachts, was Korčula's Old Town.

The dazzling spectacle of the medieval walled city could never tire me. It was placed on a bubble of land that protruded regally into the sea, and its grandeur mirrored Dubrovnik's larger old town that was some two hours' drive away. It was over twenty-five years ago since I had visited Dubrovnik, and like discovering a lost twin, I was astonished that such a similar place existed.

My first visit to Croatia had been before the Siege of Dubrovnik — the six-month conflict beginning in October 1991 between the Yugoslav People's Army and Croatian forces seeking independence. Watching the news at home, I had found it heart-breaking to imagine how such a beautiful location could be treated in such a destructive manner. Friends from the Social Club had assured me that the old walled town had been beautifully restored since the fighting, but nothing could take away my memories of those buildings in their original splendour. So, after our arrival at Dubrovnik airport, I had allowed myself just a fleeting glance of Dubrovnik's Old Town through the window of the coach.

Fortunately, the island of Korčula had escaped such a brutal bombardment, and its twee fishbone streets offered a timeless vision of wonderment and Venetian Renaissance. Holiday brochures may excite and bluster, but with a staggering backdrop of mountains, this was a vision that I could never have imagined.

As we had crossed from the mainland in a small, converted fishing boat, I had squeezed Juliet's fingers and whispered 'Thank you' in her ear.

Now Olivia cautiously peered down into the sea, but when the spray lightly grazed her pink T-shirt, she dramatically scrunched her nose and took a step backwards to emphasise how turbulent the water was. I could not deny that there was a strong current this morning, but I had the feeling that it was going to be a long and drawn-out hour before a decision was made to cancel the excursion. At least then, we could return to the hotel, and I would be rid of her. I began to make a contingency plan for my day alone. I could walk to the neighbouring village of Lumbarda, have some lunch, and then trek on to the lighthouse. This was one of the suggestions that had been made by the delightful holiday representative on our first day in Korčula. Yes, her English pronunciation might have slightly confused the route that I would need to take, but I was prepared to walk on the main road and follow the traffic signs. The meal tonight might prove to be a potential headache if Juliet didn't feel well enough to leave the hotel room. Although, I knew that I could take Olivia to the lovely beach restaurant that was close to the hotel. They served a generous selection of wood-fired pizzas, but most importantly, the live music would discourage any conversation. If I was really lucky, Olivia might want to eat a takeaway pizza in her room. I would happily venture out alone, after all, at least there would only be myself to poison.

Olivia removed her mobile phone from her rucksack and then squatted down to take a photograph of the yachts. Taking pictures appeared to be one of the few things in life that motivated her. The other things that generated mild bursts of enthusiasm were gazing out of random windows, sighing, prodding pieces of fabric, and watching reality television programmes. To her mother's consternation, I had howled with laughter when I had heard that she wanted to go to university to study psychology. Olivia could make a pet tortoise feel unloved.

Another larger boat had now caught her attention, and she

elegantly moved further along the jetty. Despite her attractive figure and facial features, it didn't surprise me that Olivia was single. But fortunately for her, personality and attitude are not clearly visible to the naked eye, and every time we visited Korčula Old Town, there was a clear transformation in her body language as she sashayed along the sidewalk. But this morning, any effort to impress potential suitors would be a waste of her time, because the yacht crews appeared to have abandoned ship. I assumed that they had taken refuge in the numerous cafes that sheltered within the historical old walls.

Of course, I was only making assumptions about her sexuality and what she perceived as attractive. It certainly made no difference to me, although her mother had once commented that her father would disinherit her if she brought a girlfriend home. It was the only time that I had felt sympathy for Olivia.

Keeping a discreet distance, I followed Olivia across the street, and after gracefully sidestepping a motorbike, she moved through the alley of buildings that snaked up to the gateway of the Old Town. I wondered if I should cheekily ask her if she wanted me to pose on the magnificent stone steps but kept my mouth shut when I saw her excitement that her cherished photograph would be tourist-free. The early hour and blustery weather seemed to have kept them at bay this morning.

This was the sheltered area of the Old Town, and I could scarcely detect any trace of the wind. I had learnt quite a lot about the town's secrets on Sunday evening, when Juliet had insisted that we all attend a demonstration of sword fighting. Despite it being an ancient ritual that was unique to the island, I had struggled to hide my scepticism. My expectations had deteriorated further, when I had been seated next to a boring man from Wolverhampton. He clearly thought that he was an expert on all things Croatian but certainly wasn't. Although, he did explain to me that some of the streets on the eastern side of the town are shaped in a small curve to protect the residents from the cold north-easterly winds. But this wasn't something that I needed to hear at the time, as the temperature was about twenty-seven degrees, and a cool breeze would have been very welcome.

The evening had begun with a curious huddle of local singers who performed four traditional Croatian songs in a tight and cosy circle. This meant that half of the group had their backs turned to the audience. Two of the female members of the choir seemed to find this as amusing as I did, because they grinned and giggled through the entire repertoire. Yet, the standard of music was good, joyous, certainly different, and well received by the audience. The mood of the evening turned darker when a large cast of dancers dressed as medieval soldiers trooped gravely into the square, and then the Moreska Sword Dance began. We were quickly swept back in time and treated to a captivating story of an abducted princess, two rival kings, war, heroism, victory and romance. Perhaps this fifteenth century battle between white and black kings — the Christians and Moors — was not a religious theme that the Authorities would dare to re-enact in the United Kingdom, but the skills and energy of the swordfighters during the seven dances were truly breath-taking. Even Olivia was impressed, and at the end of show, she insisted on having her photograph taken whilst holding one of the heavy swords. I had the feeling that *Daddy* would be absolutely delighted to see his daughter having so much fun without him. Sadly, this 'fun' was restricted to just a few fleeting moments, and her sullen expression quickly returned.

Olivia's mood swings reminded me that I had no regrets about not having children. Perhaps the closest I had been was with Sara, a ten-month relationship that I'd had during my mid-forties. It had been quite painful to let her go because she had been so keen to start a family. But children have a selfishness and dependency that make me feel so uncomfortable. Like a dog wearing a tartan coat. Having children is similar to owning a shop or a factory, and I prefer to work from a lorry that is mobile. I like to feel the freedom of being able to move on or even to disappear if I have to. Yet now I was a decade older and relatively settled in my life. I was even beginning to believe that I could live with Juliet one day, but only if her obnoxious daughter had left home.

\*\*\*

Olivia had tired of the town's glorious old steps, and after dropping her swagger, she'd bumbled her way up to the main square. The old buildings resembled an enchanting corridor of suede, their rusty red roofs the only colour. Fidgeting with her camera, Olivia peered briefly through the doorway of the Sveti Marko Cathedral, before moving on again. I followed behind, trying to be inconspicuous. Trying to be positive. For a further ten minutes, we explored the narrow and cascading streets in this peculiar and awkward manner until I finally plucked up the courage to speak. "Maybe, we should find a place to have a drink. There are plenty of nice cafés dotted about."

"Typical snooker player," she said snidely. "Old golfers wouldn't need a rest. They have something called stamina."

*Old*, I mused. "No, it's nothing to do with that. I need to use the toilet."

"That's gross!"

"Not really. I see it more as strategic thinking. There may not be a toilet on the boat."

"I'm sorry! What am I supposed to do?"

"The same as me. Think ahead and use the one in the café."

Olivia performed a strange pirouette movement before stomping past a quaint shop, its stone steps a hive of gifts and paintings.

"You're very welcome to choose the café," I called after her, as a very colourful portrait of the Old Town rocked precariously on its easel.

She refused to make a choice, stubbornly glaring down at her feet as she walked. I reluctantly suggested that we make our way down towards the sea and follow the city walls. Again, she refused to speak. Frustratedly, I dragged the bottom of my T-shirt over my stomach but decided at least we had one thing in common. I was desperately hoping that the wind had picked up and I would be able to spend the rest of the day on my own.

I found a charming café that squatted beneath the old historical walls, its haphazard cluster of outside tables sheltered between two buildings. Apart from a small grunt, Olivia made no recognisable protest, so I encouraged her to sit down on one of the quaint blue chairs and look at the menu. The door of the café was guarded by a huge ginger cat whose fur spilled over its wooden perch like treacle. Avoiding its hostile stare, I squeezed my body against the doorframe and went inside. I felt relieved to be away from Olivia for a few minutes. It reminded me of one Sunday morning when I had broken up with an ex-girlfriend. We had spent an uncomfortable evening in a local restaurant where she had made several comments about my dull choice of food — a calzone pizza — and then my uncouth eating habits as I tried to devour the 'monstrous looking thing'. After a disturbing night's sleep, it was difficult to conceal my relief when she informed me that the relationship 'was not in full working order'. Her formal manner felt more akin to a discussion with a car mechanic, except for the fact that I was wearing just my underwear. We had only been together for two months, and not for the first time, I drove away from her posh bungalow listening to *Easy* by *The Commodores*.

The interior of the café was tiny. There was a small half-moon shaped area, two tables with matching stools, and two flimsy wooden doors. One had a life-size painting of a man scrawled down it. His grey, wispy beard had an uncomfortable resemblance to my own. The other door depicted a huge vase of pink flowers. I chose the beard.

Tentatively slipping my body past the ginger cat again, I was surprised to see that Olivia was squatting behind one of the chairs, her mobile phone positioned just a few inches from the wooden spindles. "The toilets are quite respectable," I quipped naughtily. "You'll be quite safe to go in there."

She stood up quickly and cumbersomely, seemingly a little embarrassed by my sudden intrusion. "People like you will never understand art," she snapped back at me. "You're uncouth."

*Big word, probably one of Daddy's.* "I'm not one-dimensional, you know. I like snooker and music."

"Music," she repeated the word for no apparent reason.

"Yes, I like listening to music."

"More like noise," she said, checking the quality of her photograph. "I bet you like to record the sound of workmen digging holes."

I laughed. She was behaving like a demented comedian. "Sometimes, but I don't listen to it when I'm on my holidays. Have you found something that you'd like to drink? Something arty, perhaps?"

"A glass of sparkling water will be fine."

The café owner had followed me outside, so I put down my rucksack and ordered our drinks. The man shuffled his weight nervously, as if trying to neutralise the breeze that was flapping against his trousers.

"Was that one of your father's quotes?" I asked her, after the man had hurried back inside.

"Huh?"

"The delightful sounds of workmen digging holes."

"No!" she lied.

"I didn't say that I didn't like it. I might even use it at the Social Club — but before the regulars are inebriated or die of lung cancer, of course."

"You're welcome."

We sat in silence, pretending to listen to the conversation of an old French couple who had settled down on the next table. Then, after receiving our drinks, I concentrated on not slurping my latte.

"Can we go back to the hotel now?" she asked tetchily.

"I'm not sure. The problem is that the weather might be improving," I mumbled, as a gust of wind probed and then rattled a piece of loose chipboard. "But whatever we do, we need to go via the jetty on the way back."

"Why? There will be no one there."

"We don't know that. Anyway, your mother won't be happy if she's not reimbursed. We have to show willing on our part."

It took some persuasion to get Olivia to visit the toilet,

and then she stubbornly folded her arms to demonstrate her impatience about the time that it took to settle the bill. It annoyed me how disrespectful she was about money — especially *other people's money*. Her father had given her some extra pocket money to help her 'get through the holiday ordeal', but this money would only be spent on a new handbag, clothes, and Daddy's special present.

She set a quicker pace when we departed from the café, and because I was checking my mobile phone for new messages, I struggled to keep up with her.

There were no new messages.

The boats in the harbour swayed like drunks, and I wondered how the organisers of this trip must be feeling. I was self-employed and knew that a cancelled delivery would hit me hard financially. Just a few weeks ago I'd driven down to Birmingham to discover that my services were no longer required. Something to do with an unexpected bankruptcy — whatever that meant. Being just the 'little man with the van', no compensation was offered.

Olivia retraced the route by the water polo court, her head making joyous little glances towards the tempestuous sea. Yet, when the jetty came into view, she appeared to stumble. Her disappointment erupting like an Icelandic geyser.

I didn't know whether to laugh or commiserate with her.

There were five people standing on the jetty.

Olivia's change in body language reminded me of the final dramatic scene of Sunday evening's sword dance, when the mortally wounded Black King had slumped to the dusty courtyard, and the princess had rushed back into the arms of her one true love. Olivia's walking pace dribbled to a standstill, and I nearly clattered into the back of her.

"We just need to make our presence known," I said encouragingly.

Perhaps she was in a trance, but her legs staggered onwards.

Like a flock of sheep, there is something quite distinctive about a group of tourists waiting for the start of an excursion. Perhaps it's their multi-coloured shorts, their upmarket sunglasses, and their bulging bags that tease the coarse strands of a worn beach towel. Or maybe, it's the edgy stance that they adopt to ensure that a discreet three-foot canyon of space is left between themselves and the next stranger. Their eyes watched and scrutinised us, and I felt like a rebellious heifer that had escaped the herd.

I was approached by an elegant young blonde lady. "You don't look like a 'Juliet'," she said, trying to hide the concern in her voice. She had a zealous face with blue eyes, a cute, tipped nose, and freckles that were scattered like daisies.

"I'm not a Romeo either. But this is Juliet's daughter, and my name is Craig."

"Right . . . Okay. It's a pleasure to meet you. I'm the organiser, Amy."

"Sorry, that was rubbish," I apologised. "Let me explain. Unfortunately, Juliet is unwell. I was always on the guest list, but Olivia is taking her mother's place."

Amy exhaled loudly. "That's absolutely fine. I'm very sorry to hear about Juliet, though."

"It's just one of those annoying holiday bugs. I'm sure that she'll be back to full strength by tomorrow morning."

"Unless you poison her again," Olivia mumbled far too loudly.

Amy had already turned away to address the group. She appeared to have enough problems to deal with, and a potential murderer was low on her priorities. "I don't know if Mario will be able to pick us up from here," she said sternly. "But don't worry, he knows exactly what he is doing out there."

I'm not sure what size or shape of vessel my imagination had been expecting, but it wasn't anything like the small boat that was about two hundred yards offshore. A small boat that was clearly struggling to find a suitable route to reach us. It looked like the sort of craft that would be used by anglers on a fishing trip, or at best, a water taxi. I could see a simple blue cabin and then a short space at the rear for its passengers. There were seven of us on the jetty, and the boat's maximum capacity must have been ten persons.

Amy was on her mobile phone now, her eyes fixed on the blue

bobbing object that resembled a wild horse at a rodeo. "Oh," she said, her hand falling away to rest on her waist, "Mario suggests that we walk around the corner. There's a more sheltered jetty that he will try to reach instead. It's not that far."

None of the sheep questioned this command. They shuffled their legs, adjusted the straps of their belongings, and set off to follow her.

Olivia was far less accepting of the situation. "This is absolutely fucking ridiculous," she grunted in my ear. "You must do something! You need to save these stupid peoples' lives!"

"The boat has already travelled from somewhere," I pointed out, "so I don't think it's a life or death situation."

"Typical! Daddy would have made a stand."

"Look, your mother set her heart on this trip. It's your choice, but I'm not going back to the hotel to try and explain to her why the boat left without me."

"Well, I won't be the one whimpering like a baby when the boat capsizes."

I ignored her and followed the group. After half an hour in Olivia's company, our fellow passengers might be more than willing to take their chances in the choppy water.

# CHAPTER THREE

The air temperature was rising sharply in the sheltered areas. If the wind was to drop in the afternoon, then the heat could well reach the mid-thirties, and it might be uncomfortable on the small boat. Since our arrival in Croatia, Olivia had appeared to be quite naïve about the danger of direct sunlight. Whilst sitting by the pool, she often shuffled her sun lounger away from the shadows like a marshmallow hovering over a campfire. I was surprised that she hadn't suffered from sunstroke. *Not that I expected her mood would suffer.*

Predictably, Olivia was now positioned at the rear of our curious posse, discarding her glamourous demeanour to sulkily drag her feet behind me. I followed a gruff looking man who was probably in his early sixties. He had straggly grey hair that merged into his beard. As he turned his head, it looked like all his hair was a single living creature — a bit like a onesie. His companion was perhaps a little younger. She was small, with short snow-white hair and feverish eyes. I couldn't decide who the other male was. He was probably in his late twenties, wiry in shape, with a shaven head. Occasionally, he would veer across the path to chat to the small woman, but this might have been through friendliness and not because they were related or friends.

The final member of the group was almost certainly a lone traveller. She stayed close to Amy's side, her broad and slightly cumbersome shoulders rocking as she bounced awkwardly along the road. She could only have been in her thirties, but it was clear that walking wasn't one of her favourite pastimes.

We had reached a crossroads. The route to our hotel was

straight on, but Amy veered left, and her feet quickly disappeared as she strode down a steep hill. Olivia groaned loudly behind me. The sound reminded me of my neighbour's dog when it was hungry.

I could see that there were three small boats moored at the jetty, and one of them was the blue boat that Amy had been in contact with on her mobile phone. The sea was far calmer here, which wasn't lost on Olivia. "Great!" she hissed. "We're just going to sail around this stupid cove all day. I could've just watched you from the hotel pool."

*Bet you wouldn't have waved at us, though.* I noticed that Amy was enthusiastically greeting a tall young man dressed in a black T-shirt. It did seem unlikely that the trip would have to be abandoned, and we would return to the hotel.

"This is Mario," Amy explained. "And this is Mario's boat. Let's get onboard and introduce ourselves."

"We're only going on a shitty boat, love," Olivia muttered sarcastically. "It's not a bloody bible meeting."

I closed my eyes tightly and prayed for any passing God to save me.

Amy expertly hopped onto the boat, and the rest of us formed an impromptu line as we waited for Mario to guide us onboard.

As I had anticipated, the boat was a basic design with wooden seats set in a crushed semi-circle with a crude rectangle block in the middle. The cabin looked like a garden shed with its backwall missing. I made my way to the rear of the boat and selected a seat near the snowy-haired older lady. I did notice a strange metal contraption directly behind my head, but at least if I took this seat it was unlikely to interfere with Olivia. Heaven knows what she would have made of it. Olivia was surprisingly complacent at the moment, although her face held a vindictive teenage expression that gleefully proclaimed: *I told you that this was a complete joke, the boat is a fleapit and I'm going to watch you squirm.*

There was a nervous silence as we watched Mario drop down onto his knees and rummage around on the floor of his 'shed'. I almost expected him to emerge with a rusting can of creosote, yet after making a few strange whistling sounds, he crawled towards us holding a large plastic bottle of red liquid and a stack of plastic cups. He carelessly plonked them down on the middle block, his white teeth gleaming from his tanned face.

I thought that I had probably been on the right lines with the creosote, and he was going to use the plastic cups to pour some sort of oil into the boat's engine, but instead, like a hippie, he made himself comfortable on the floor. "So, this is a wine trip — yes?" he asked us jovially. "Then let's start the day in the right way."

*Wine?* I stared disbelievingly at the large plastic bottle. It looked like it had once contained lemonade.

"Mario makes his own wine," Amy gushed excitedly. "I assume it's not too early to enjoy a tipple?"

"It's never too early," said the older woman. Her voice had a lush Irish lilt.

There was a subtle and welcome change in Olivia's demeanour the moment that Mario handed out the plastic cups. I had been a little worried about the wine tasting element of the trip, although it hadn't stopped her drinking so far. Besides, she was nearly eighteen. Juliet had raised the same concern during our first evening meal in Korčula. 'I've brought along my fake ID, Stupid,' Olivia had helpfully informed her mother.

I didn't know if it had something to do with the delayed start to our excursion, but Mario was very generous with his portions. He cheerily splashed his creation into our cups and encouraged us to drink it. Olivia duly obliged. For the first time that morning, I saw the scaffold of a smile on her lips. But perhaps this was only because the wine tasted so fantastic.

"Now we should be in the mood for a few introductions," Amy said, raising her cup towards the shed's roof as if it was some sort of temple. "But don't worry, I'll go first." She took two short breaths, almost like she was having a little meditation. "Thank you so much for joining us today. You may have noticed that I'm more of an adopted Croatian, and my home country is England — or to be more precise, a little town in Cambridgeshire. But once you have discovered Korčula, it is very tempting to stay. And so here I am today!" There was some polite acknowledgement and some genuine envy from the group. "Mario is very much a local, though," Amy continued, "and just like his lovely boat, he knows these islands intimately. You are in very safe hands."

"Yes, it is true," Mario cried. "My boat even sneaks out at night when I am fast asleep!"

Amy laughed. "This is certainly a very magical place."

Their patter was so slick that I couldn't decide if they were following a script or if Mario had delivered this joke for the first time.

"Okay, over to you," Amy said, folding her arms to make the point that she had completed her opening address.

"My name is Anna," said the other young woman, "and as you can tell from my accent, I've travelled here all the way from Sydney in Australia!"

"Yes, it's quite remarkable," Amy agreed, "and as you were telling me earlier, you're here for about three weeks?"

"Yeah, just over three weeks. I've come up the coast from Dubrovnik, but sadly, I'm leaving Croatia in two days' time."

"Are you going anywhere else in Europe?"

"Nope . . . but yeah, maybe I should have planned that," Anna said, a little uncertainly. "But geez, the Europeans have it made with the quick two-hour flights. It's such a long way back to Sydney."

"We popped over from Belfast," the older lady joined the conversation. "I'm Grace, this is my husband, Frank, and my son, Sean."

"But I flew in from London," Sean said, before adding pointedly, "because London is my home now."

Frank sighed heavily.

"We're also from England," I said dolefully. "Craig and Olivia."

"Oh no, not the Irish and the English on one small boat!" Mario quipped. "Hope you're going to get along today?"

"We'll see." Frank muttered. He was just like his voice, surly and bristly.

"Um, so are you father and daughter?" Amy asked quickly.

"Absolutely not," Olivia said with dismay. "He's just briefly hanging out with my poor mother."

# CHAPTER FOUR

We departed from the jetty with a loud plop and a retching splutter, bobbing up and down for a short distance before twisting at a peculiar angle and then drifting sideways in the current. I wondered if the boat was drowning.

"Good job we're not a space shuttle," Mario quipped. He disappeared further into his shed and poked some sort of lever. After another plopping sound and a waft of smoke, the boat veered back on course and we were sailing away from the jetty. This time we kept moving, the pitter patter of the propeller droning behind me.

"We're away," Amy cried with obvious relief. "Once we get around the headland, there's a gorgeous secluded bay where we will make our first stop."

There was a little bit of turbulence in the water, but nothing like the strong current that I had expected. *This is actually going to happen,* I resigned myself. *I'm trapped on this dilapidated boat with Olivia, an Irishman who despises me, and a crazy sailor.*

We were sailing towards the thickly wooded peninsula that housed our hotel, the magnificent Old Town on our left. I was captivated by its blaze of red roofs, its prominence, and the imperial manner in which it was projected into the bay. Perhaps it's an age thing but I simply couldn't help but comment on its splendour. "It's just so glorious," my voice gushed. "I can't imagine how the island would look if the old buildings weren't there."

"You mean like a boil," Olivia said lazily.

My body rocked and vibrated. "A what?"

She sighed. "You know — a spot on your face. It's troubling you, and you're desperate to know what your face would look like if the boil was lanced."

"Not really, but it's an interesting take on the situation. Do young people always compare everything in the world to beauty and fashion?"

"No! It's only because old people have no imagination."

I didn't want to continue this conversation in such a confined and public space yet felt that I needed to make at least one important point. "I am younger than your father," I whispered.

"Huh. But he's got class."

The young man smiled and turned his gaze back to the Old Town.

Our little vessel was forced to grapple and tussle in the rough sea beyond the headland. But as we made a sharp turn towards the ferry port, the water appeared to yawn and lapse into a calmer mood. Using Olivia's logic and imagination, the ugly ferry port was another 'boil' on the island. However, it was tucked away, and its functionality clearly outweighed its appearance. Without its presence, the island would struggle to cater for the locals and the huge number of summer tourists. We had been lucky on our arrival and had not needed the large and cumbersome ferry. After the long journey from Dubrovnik airport, the minibus had dropped us off on a tiny jetty on the mainland. We had gawked at our first view of the imperious Old Town and then the small fishing boat that was coming to collect us. It was a truly magical moment. 'A Mamma Mia moment,' Juliet had noted.

***

The sporadic rocking of the boat reminded me of my relationships with women. People sometimes refer to having a 'type', and although it sounds strange, I suppose mine would be the *divorced* woman. Perhaps I was attracted to their vulnerability, their uncertainty, and their availability. Like a concrete jetty, I felt that my own life was fixed, stable, and under my control; yet having witnessed my parents' divorce I was aware of the emotional desolation and helplessness that can be inflicted. I genuinely understood and cared about the turmoil that was happening in these women's lives. The problem was — and there was clearly a pattern — that women treated me like a short-term fix before moving on. *Was it me?* Or was this just a symptom of their circumstances, and my role was to always be a stopgap? But all these relationships had ended amicably, and generally, I had felt equally happy to move on.

Except for one relationship — Penny.

This relationship continued to haunt my dreams, and yet, it seemed so silly. We had never even kissed.

***

We followed the bumbling coastline down to Lumbarda, with Amy nervously breaking the silence to point out the charming properties that delicately crouched on the shallow clifftop. With the warm and sheltered sea just a few feet below the bottom of their gardens, you couldn't help but compare it to the fluster of city life. I wondered if this was how mankind was supposed to live and function.

Nuzzled up inside a cove, the tiny community of Lumbarda was equally as idyllic. I was delighted to see that Olivia had reached for her mobile phone and was now aiming the built-in camera at a church that hugged the rocky landscape above the bay.

"We could walk to this village later in the week," I suggested.

"What's the point of that?"

"It's a lovely place to visit."

"We've seen it now."

"I meant for your mother's benefit."

Olivia sighed heavily. She was getting good at this today. "Why do you think I'm taking this photograph?"

There was a tiny, uninhabited island to our left. It was a mosaic of rocks, turquoise water and dishevelled trees. The spindly branches loitered, suspicious, wily, hands in pockets, like bemused castaways. Mario cut the engine and casually tossed the boat's anchor into the deep clear water. Amy picked up a damp cardboard box from the floor and placed it between us. "Our first swim stop," she said excitedly. "Help yourself to the equipment."

Anna needed no further encouragement and immediately delved into the box. She made a peculiar little grunt and plucked out a bright blue mask and snorkel, before sliding the container politely towards us.

Olivia squirmed, and then using one outstretched finger, she prodded the box away from her.

"Suit yourself," said the Australian as she plunged ineptly over the side of the boat.

The Irish family had less qualms, and treating the box like a Christmas hamper, they cheerfully made their selections based on design and size.

To Olivia's consternation, I had brought along my own mask and snorkel, and now I lovingly unravelled it from my towel. The equipment was nearly twenty-years old now and had been an expensive purchase from a diving shop. I had never had any desire to swim more than a few feet below the surface, but the shop had been part of a delivery I'd been assigned to and the owner had been a very good salesman. Despite my doubts at the time, it had proved to be a wonderful acquisition that I had never regretted. There are plenty of masks on sale at the seaside, but the majority will leave you with a soggy face and itchy eyes.

It was a relief to leave the boat, and I didn't care if my entry into the water was undignified. Once your masked face dips beneath the surface, you are transported into a bewildering domain that offers an exhilarating freedom. And here, in the depths beyond the shore, the experience was intensified; the clear water providing an endless spectacle of brilliant colours and patterns. It was a magical and alien world, breached only by the apologetic movement of limbs and the sound of my breathing. Eventually raising my head, I saw that Olivia had been shamed into entering the water. Still shunning the mask and snorkel, she had climbed to the bottom of the ladder, her neck stretched cumbersomely as she desperately tried to keep her hair dry. I turned and swam far away from her, dreading the moment that I'd have to return.

*\*\**

Fish have always fascinated me.

My first memory takes me back to a tropical fish tank in the waiting area of a local Chinese restaurant. I must have been about ten years old because my parents had just separated, and my flustered father could not cook. We made the same short journey to collect our takeaway for five consecutive Saturday evenings. The fish tank was pristine, the kitchen much less so. To my huge disappointment, after a visit from a food and hygiene inspector, the restaurant was closed down. My father tried to console me by driving further up the road to a tiny shop that served Indian cuisine. I quickly took a liking to the food, but I missed the tropical fish. The compromise was a couple of goldfish. When I was given permission to eat my food next to the big glass fishbowl in my father's living room, the Indian food tasted even better.

The fish that I was now following through the warm Adriatic Sea was four times the size of *Gavin* and *Garry Goldfish*. And more courageous. It amused me how this Croatian fish refused to be fazed by my presence, ignoring my cumbersome swimming to continue elegantly on its journey. I was so engrossed by its indifference that my head clumsily clattered into a slaying arm. "So sorry!" I spluttered, after raising my head above the water.

"Don't worry, I get along with the English just fine," Sean said, tugging his mask up onto his forehead. "And I'd much rather spend some time with my father in a beautiful place like this than return to dreary Belfast."

"It rains in Yorkshire, too," I said. "Where are you staying on the island?"

"Oh, a wonderful place. It's an apartment on the other side of the Old Town, about a fifteen-minute walk down the coastal road."

"You sound like a regular."

"No, not at all. It's my first visit to the island. Korčula was recommended to me by a very good friend." He wiped a few droplets of seawater from his eyes and ineptly pulled his mask down over his nose. Then, he carried on doing his thing in the water. I wondered if fish occasionally took a break from their swimming and shared similar pleasantries.

I wasn't someone who spent a lot of my time on organised holiday excursions, but I now became aware of that awkward moment when you try and decide if this was the polite moment *to return to the coach*. Olivia and Grace were already back onboard, and Frank was hauling his large flabby stomach up the ladder. I didn't wish to appear to be racing Sean back to the boat, so I casually trod water for a few moments and looked around for Anna.

It took a few head turns before I spotted her, and it was immediately obvious that she was far more proficient at gliding through the water than moving on dry land. And, unlike the rest of us, she had no hesitation in diving deep beneath the water if she spotted something of interest. She seemed to be in no rush to return to the boat, so I decided to swim across to the anchor and look at the spot where it was buried into the seabed. The answer was unremarkable — a sandy and lonely grave — but it did give me a few more peaceful minutes in the warm and glorious sea.

# CHAPTER FIVE

I was aware of the heat as soon as my shoulders emerged from the water, and I began my precarious ascent up the boat's metal ladder. The wind had dropped to a gentle breeze, and like the prodding of invisible fingers, I could feel a burning sensation across my back.

Olivia was leaning over the side of the boat, her mobile phone artistically pointing down at the sea. I slipped past her and picked up my towel. "Did you enjoy that?" I asked reluctantly, as she swung her body in my direction.

"I'm sure I was attacked by something horrible," she answered grumpily.

"It's not Australia," Amy reassured her. "You'll be safe from sharks here."

"Our bull sharks are like puppy dogs!" shouted a voice from the ladder. "It's the box jellyfish you need to look out for. Not forgetting the southern blue-lined octopus, the Sydney funnel-web spider, the common death adder, and then there's the crafty old crocs."

"Would that be the saltwater kind?" Sean asked curiously.

"Sure is. Got one hell of a temper if you try and cuddle it."

"I thought you only cuddled the koala bear."

Anna plodded towards her seat, shaking her wet hair like a Great Dane. "Are you kidding? They stink of rotting vegetation."

I saw Mario smiling wickedly as he twisted the lid on his magical lemonade container. "My little boat would need a standby emergency crew if I worked in Australia. There wouldn't be any room for the tourists."

"That wouldn't matter," I said, joining the conversation, "the tourists would all have been eaten."

"And that's a bad thing?" Frank grunted.

"No," Mario agreed.

When you make the booking for your summer holiday, your imagination drools about moments like this. A boat moored next to a desert island, bright sunshine and a clear turquoise ocean. And then there was the wine — Mario's very special homemade wine.

"Now that we've covered the beautiful, although, perhaps a little disturbing, Australia," Amy said, "is there anything that you'd like to know about Korčula?"

"Oh, lots of things," Grace said eagerly, "many things. But you know, it is so annoying, because I just can't think of them now. This amazing wine is certainly not helping my brain!"

"I know exactly what you mean, but we do have all day. I can tell you that the island is approximately twenty-nine miles in length and five miles wide. The population is about seventeen thousand, but this increases considerably during the tourist season."

"Food!" Grace's voice sang out. She sounded like she was auditioning for a musical. "Yes, I wanted to ask you about the local dishes we should try."

"That's a lovely question. There's black risotto. Most of the seafood restaurants have this on the menu. And strukli. You should all try this. It's a delicious pastry filled with cottage cheese and sour cream."

"And what about the language," Sean said. "I feel useless when I travel abroad, but Mario's English is exceptionally good. I've noticed this with many of the locals."

"Yes, and my English isn't bad either," Amy quipped. "Fortunately, a large proportion of Croatians are multilingual. I think they also speak some German and Italian. Is that right, Mario?"

"Nein!" he said, raising his plastic cup.

"I've got a question," Frank said. "Was Korčula attacked by the

Serbian army during the Croatian War of Independence?"

"No," Mario said sternly. "*Next question.*"

"But surely the enemy's ships had to sail down this coast during the siege of Dubrovnik? Didn't anyone notice them?"

Mario shrugged and turned away.

"And . . . and the island has a dense forest," Amy said uneasily, "and because of this, the ancient Greeks called the island: Black Korčula. Is there anything . . ."

"Yes." The voice belonged to Olivia. "I have a question for Mario."

I cringed.

"Go ahead," Amy encouraged her.

"Do you put up a tree on Christmas Eve?"

Mario laughed loudly and spun around to face her. "Yes, of course I put up a Christmas tree. I'm Catholic and not a practising Jedi! No, thank you, that is a good question to ask, and just so you know, I do like the Star Wars movies. Don't you?"

"No," Olivia said petulantly. "I don't get them. They're just really silly."

# CHAPTER SIX

The boat shuffled against the current, its movement harmonised with its tipsy passengers. After a further cup of Mario's wine, the alcohol had blurred the sun's warmth, hugging, and then smothering our heads and shoulders. Mario was leaning manically inside his shed, urging the boat to turn one hundred and eighty degrees. "Don't worry," Amy reassured us, "we're on our way to Badija."

It made me think that divorced women are like the sea. They share the same unpredictable moods and volatility. And, where children are involved, I'm always amazed at the incredible pace at which changes are made to the 'happy family home'. In my opinion, the most unsubtle and disturbing parts of this process are the transformations made to the photograph albums and the pictures on the wall — poor daddy is immediately extinguished. I'm not sure if the mothers are aware of the psychological damage inflicted on the children, and quite possibly, themselves. I do try to hold my tongue, but you quickly get the feeling that some of these women will bear the scars forever. An invisible rage, bitterness, and mistrust will seep into new relationships and cause an ongoing cycle of destruction.

But with Penny, it was just the opposite. The photographs of her ex-husband adorned her rented home with pride, and at first, I had assumed that she was a widow. A mutual friend had recommended me to Penny, because of my house removal services and perhaps my potential as a confidant. Dare I even think — lover. I had certainly felt an instant and overwhelming attraction. To this day, she still invades my dreams, and I hope that she will always continue to do so. Penny was standing on the pavement when I pulled up in my lorry, her hair long and alluringly black, her blue eyes large and penetrating. 'You'll do,' she had said audaciously. 'You'll do very nicely.' But I had never understood what this meant, even at the point I had panicked and backed away from her.

"What a wonderful spectacle." Grace broke my thoughts.

I turned and followed her gaze.

Two things dominated the small island of Badija, its dense forest and a monastery. The forest seethed and ravaged the landscape like a badly fitted wig, whereas the monastery bowed majestically at the water's edge, a leopard drinking from a stream. Yet, there was something else. Something aloof and forbidding about its posture.

Amy raised her hand and cleared her throat, so we knew that some interesting information was about to follow. The boat hushed, and she spoke to us slowly, like a chemistry teacher explaining the periodic table:

"The Franciscan monastery was built around the fourteenth century after the officials of Korčula Town had donated the island to the Franciscans of Bosnia. In later years, the building was used as a boy's grammar school, before it was taken over and closed in 1943 by the Communist authorities. An odd fifty years of muddled activity then followed, where the monastery was used as a sports centre and a hostel. Then, in 2003, the new Croatian Government took over the island and returned it back to the original owners. At the present time, the monastery is being repaired so that it can once again become a religious, cultural, and educational centre. The monks have returned!"

"And so they should," Grace said appreciatively. "Good for them."

As I stared at the building, I couldn't help but wonder if the island was hiding darker secrets from those strange Communist years. Mario also had his eyes fixed on the monastery, but he was eerily silent. He clearly had no desire to add anything further to Amy's short and rigid history lesson.

"We're going to stop here for about thirty minutes," Amy said, completing her speech. "You can walk to the monastery or just pop to the toilet in the café. But do keep a look out for the friendly deer."

Our boat moored at a skinny jetty next to a bright red and white commercial vessel that was curiously called: *Fish Supper*. I couldn't help but smile at the boat's decorative tables and seating area. If pirates had takeaway restaurants, then perhaps this is what they would look like.

As I tentatively placed my feet on the concrete, my body felt crushed by the heat of the sun. You could almost hear the crackle of the dry branches that formed a dense and intimidating throng a few metres from the shore. "We can use the water taxi to visit the monastery on another day," I said to Olivia. "I'm sure your mother would like it here."

Silence.

"Good." I nodded my head. "But for now, shall we just 'pop to the toilet' as Amy so wonderfully described it?"

"You can," she said indignantly. "At your age, it's probably a good idea to take every opportunity. What's this now, your third visit this morning?"

"At least," I baited her. "And if I was younger, I'd have also gone in the sea."

"Gross."

It was obvious that Amy had not frequented the sea either, because she scuttled past me and made a sharp right turn at the jetty. I followed her to a rough path that was created by broken stones and pebbles, my training shoes skidding on the uneven surface. I wondered if the monks walked barefooted around the island, and the spiky path was a deliberate deterrent from the lure of salty crisps and fizzy drinks.

Such had been her haste, Amy was already standing in a short queue at the rear of the café. There was only one toilet and its crude design was similar to Mario's shed. "You didn't tell us that the toilet was so luxurious," I teased her.

"I didn't dare," she agreed. "But on the plus side, you can sneak in without buying anything from the café."

"I see. So the owners refused to offer you a commission if you encouraged the tourists to spend money there?"

She frowned. "No chance of that after they'd seen the size of Mario's boat. It would be more like having a personal shopper!"

Olivia was strangely enthused on my return to the jetty. Leaping from one foot to the other, she was pointing her mobile telephone at something concealed behind an old and bedraggled tree. "It's huge," she shrieked, "and it just keeps staring at me."

"Is it a rock?" I asked sarcastically.

"*No!* It's a deer."

I tiptoed up to her side. There was a large red deer. It had ferocious looking antlers and a bemused grizzly face. "You'll never get it through airport customs."

"I don't want to."

"Would you like a biscuit?"

"*Huh?* I'm not a child."

"I meant so you could feed the biscuit to your new friend." She watched me with curiosity as I swung the rucksack from my back and squatted down in the rubble.

"You're not intending to shove the biscuit down your pants again, are you?"

I laughed. "Why would I do that?"

"Because I've seen you ram chunks of bread inside your swimming trunks before you walk into the sea."

She knew very well that I used the bread to attract the fish when I went snorkelling. It was the easiest place to store it when I was swimming. But I was quite happy to keep our conversation going. "I put the bread there because I don't want to get my socks wet. Old men have to keep up a certain macho image, you know."

"That's just so weird. Daddy would never say anything so crude."

I removed the pack of emergency ginger biscuits that I had purchased from the supermarket on the day of our arrival. "Well, we're all different."

"*Very.*"

Tugging a couple of biscuits from the top of the packet, I held out my hand to show the deer my peaceful intentions, and then cautiously moved towards it. I wasn't entirely confident, but its antlers looked more intimidating than its long rubbery mouth. "Does your friend have a name?"

"Desmond."

"Nice. I like that. The name has a friendly ring to it." I thoughtlessly ducked my head to peer at Desmond's undercarriage, but I had no idea what I was expecting to find.

"Are you looking for a pair of socks?" she asked cheekily.

"I'm sure that Desmond has more class." The animal looked at me dolefully and then ungraciously lunged towards my hand. Fortunately, I felt nothing more than a sloppy sponge-like sensation as its tongue greedily extracted the treats. I guessed that the deer must have performed this act several times before and had probably learnt that it was not in his best interests to cause any pain. "Would you like to take a photograph of the two of us together?"

"No, because one of you is weird, and the other might get traumatised by the experience."

"I'll be fine."

Desmond was far from traumatised. His long tongue gleefully slathered over his lips, and he gawkily stretched out his chin. He wanted another ginger biscuit.

Holding my hands safely above my head to show that there were no more treats, I slowly began to back away. But the deer followed me. Desmond was no fool, he knew where my biscuits were hidden, and it was now a frantic race to reach the rucksack first. Luckily, I was just a little bit closer. My hand plunged into the bag at the same time as my feet stumbled, and like a commando, I grabbed a handful of biscuits and released a hail of ginger bullets as I crashed onto the ground. Stifling a groan, I dragged my rucksack to safety behind the old tree, and Desmond joyously ate his rewards.

"Is this what attracts my poor mother to you?" Olivia laughed. "Free ginger biscuits."

I rubbed my knees and leaned back against the trunk. "You'd have to ask her," I said. "Maybe its down to my special relationship with animals."

"Yes, that must be it. *Special*."

It was a few minutes later when I became aware of the itch.

At first, I thought it was due to the ragged shape of the tree, and I adjusted my posture to peer around the trunk.

Desmond had seemingly forgotten about the rucksack and was scouring the ground for pieces of biscuit. *An honourable victory*, I congratulated myself, except I couldn't ignore the feeling that something strange was happening to my back. I had landed on my knees when I had stumbled, so it seemed unlikely that I'd injured my upper torso, yet now the itch had spread to my arms and shoulders. I pushed myself up onto my feet and manically scratched my body. Then I felt the bite. "*Ouch!*" I cried far too loudly.

Olivia gawked at me.

Then I felt another bite.

"I'm under attack!" I shouted, desperately trying to wrestle my T-shirt over my head. My skin was still sweaty from my swim and I was forced to contort my elbows to pull my arms through the sleeves. Eventually, I was free, and I recklessly flung the T-shirt to the ground. To my horror, it was covered in a red and ugly swarm of insects. "Bloody ants!" I cried, frantically dusting my skin with my fingers. "Ants! They're everywhere!"

"Offer them a biscuit," Olivia said, before collapsing into a fit of giggles.

Ignoring her advice, I grabbed the T-shirt and ran towards the sea. My feet skidding across the pebbles like a lunatic.

I suppose if you do have to be semi-naked and covered in red blotches, it does help when you are waist deep in turquoise water and the air temperature is in the mid-thirties. But I was in no hurry to return to the shore or put my T-shirt back on. It was soaking wet because I had tried to drown the *little bastards,* and I now used the garment to dab the infected areas of skin.

The Australian lady was swimming expertly on her back thirty yards out from the shore, and I could see that the Irish couple were sauntering back from the monastery, their son trailing behind them. I assumed that Amy was already back on the boat.

Olivia crunched her feet on the pebbles as she made her way down to the sea. "Is the pantomime over now?" she called out. "I just wish that I'd filmed it."

"None of this would have happened if you hadn't introduced me to your greedy mate, Desmond."

"Oh, so it's my fault that you have this *special* relationship with the local wildlife?"

I reluctantly pulled the soggy T-shirt back over my head. I hoped that it would soothe the burning sensation on my skin and hide the wounds from the hot and groping sun. "Perhaps not entirely, but at least I've shown you that nature is unpredictable."

"Strange that these things don't happen to the television presenters." She suddenly bucked her head and raised her right hand. "*Hold on a minute!* What do you mean by 'shown me'? That's way too creepy and lecherous. You'd better not be thinking I'm your surrogate daughter!"

# CHAPTER SEVEN

With our hands placed neatly on bare knees like schoolchildren, we were sitting on the boat's wooden benches when Amy told us about the next part of the trip.

"We're going to head out a short distance to the tiny island in front of us," she explained. "The snorkelling in the deep clear water is amazing and whilst you enjoy your second swim, Mario will prepare our lunch."

"Scampi and chips!" Sean said. "Yummy."

"You're on the wrong boat," Mario grunted.

"The wrong planet," Frank added drily.

We weaved through three yachts that were anchored at different angles in the bay. The surface of the water was sheltered here, and the abandoned, locked-down vessels, lazed in the shape of cats — compact, symmetrical, paws tucked beneath their bodies. Mario cut the engine when we were about twenty-five metres from the island, and once again, the damp cardboard box was dragged out from the shed and masks were politely handed around.

"Which one are you using?" Sean asked Olivia, after exchanging a purple mask with his mother.

"Oh, I don't do it," Olivia mumbled awkwardly. "I'll just have a swim."

"You know, I used to say exactly the same thing. But as this is a snorkelling trip, you should have a go."

"He's right," Grace agreed. "We couldn't get him to enter the water and now he's like the little scampi themselves."

"Yes, but it was my mother who was supposed to be on the

trip," Olivia tried to explain. "I'm not meant to be here."

"But fate brought you to Mario's little vessel, and your life changed forever," Sean said dramatically. "Come on, I'll show you."

Olivia's rigid posture refused to buckle as Sean delved back inside the box. Then, when he pulled out a bright tangerine mask, her grim expression soured even further.

"Maybe not," he said, deftly reading her mood. "But hold on, look at this one. Doesn't it just scream reluctant aquatic?"

"Better," Olivia said grudgingly as another piece of equipment appeared.

"Much better. Go on, give it a try," Sean said encouragingly.

I was astonished to watch her tug the teal coloured mask over her hair.

"That really suits you, girl. Now we're ready to rumble."

I opened my rucksack as the two of them followed Grace towards the ladder. "Don't forget your bread," I cheekily called out.

Olivia turned and forced her lips into a smile.

***

The mazy colours of the sea were glorious. Pigments of warmth, lethargy, and summer. I swam in a straight line away from the boat, only stopping when I had reached the island.

It was difficult to imagine that anything would live on such a small island, and I wondered whether during the high winter tides some of it would be submerged. A rodent would struggle to swim across from Badija, although it wasn't impossible for an insect to be swept across in a strong current. Likewise, birds sometimes carry live food in their beaks, and the odd lizard might be lucky enough to escape. But then what? How long would it survive? The trees mirrored the rough terrain. Scraggy and doleful branches that looked like castaways. They reminded me of myself.

Perhaps I had lived on my own for too long, and once Olivia had used Daddy's money to buy a flat, I should consider moving in with Juliet. But was it too late? Was I already entrenched in a sad bachelor existence? Was this the reason that I had turned away from Penny without even a 'goodbye'?

The fish were getting smaller as the water became shallower, so I made a clumsy turn and swam back towards the boat. Sean and Olivia were snorkelling close together, their heads face down in the sea. I could see his arms occasionally rise sharply and then fall again as he pointed out a fish or other things that might excite her. I was certain that he was only interested in Olivia because he wanted some time away from his parents. It seemed likely that he had been the one who had chosen this excursion, and perhaps he had felt a little disappointed when his mother and father had come along. The family all seemed very comfortable swimming in the water, though, and even more so after a glass of wine.

I was surprised to see that Amy was also in the sea, the Australian lady effortlessly circling her like a great white shark. Anna gave the impression that she was single and appeared very content in her own company. Her personality seemed to be different from the type of lady that I had dated, and I wondered if this was because of her lifestyle. Maybe divorced women were moulded into a similar type because they endured the same kind of experiences — betrayal, hurt, secrecy, and the slow torture of witnessing pleasantries and communication shatter into a thousand pieces.

I accidentally bumped into Olivia and quickly apologised. Surprisingly, she seemed unconcerned about me breaching her personal space. "Snorkelling is brilliant, isn't it?" she gushed.

I adjusted my mask and swept my hands through the clear turquoise water. "It's wonderful. I'm glad that you're enjoying the experience."

"The colours of the fish are amazing. I wish I had my camera with me."

"I know, and sadly, it's not something you can replicate in the cold and murky river back home."

She glanced in the direction of Sean, who was now swimming with his mother. "Sean's boyfriend wasn't allowed to come on holiday with him. I think it's got something to do with his father." She hesitated. "That's unfair, isn't it?"

"Yes," I said. "I think so. Don't you?"

"Mmm . . . I guess."

"Sean mentioned to me earlier that a good friend had recommended Korčula as a holiday destination. Maybe that was actually his boyfriend?"

"What? That makes the situation even worse. Sean is so nice and earns lots of money in the city. He works in insurance or something like that." She hesitated. "You won't say anything to Sean about our chat, will you?"

"Of course not," I promised her. "I won't even tell your mother."

Her lips formed an appeased smile beneath the cloudy glass of her mask, and then she slowly submerged into the water. That eerie and secluded world she had now become a part of.

*\*\**

Mario had been busy during our absence. The curious metal contraption that had rattled behind my head as we sailed had now been transformed into a barbeque. He was diligently grilling fish on it.

"It's Master Chef," Frank grunted, wiping droplets of water from his chin.

"Bet you didn't catch anything?" Mario replied.

"Nothing that I could eat."

I squeezed past Olivia and a crude table that had been set up in the middle of the boat. Amy was juggling some plates in the shed.

"Are we going to eat shark?" Sean teased the chef.

"No, crocodile," Mario responded. "Why do you think I didn't join you for a swim?"

"Well it's a bloody small croc you're cooking!" Anna quipped.

We ate sea bream with a slice of lemon, tomato and goat's cheese. Unsurprisingly, the meal was handsomely supported by a couple of plastic cups of homemade wine. Then, after we had finished, we tossed the fish skins over the side of the boat and watched the gulls devour the remains. With the gentle rocking of the boat, the hot sun, and the warm green-blue sea, it was a surreal and utopian moment that would always remain with me.

"Have any of you visited Croatia before?"

"Poreč," Sean said, obstinately flipping back his head to finish his wine. "I went on holiday there with a good friend of mine. A wonderful friend who *loves* coming to Croatia."

Grace sighed heavily and then stared down at her bare feet.

"I've been to Dubrovnik," I said hurriedly. "I was working there."

"Doing what exactly?" Olivia asked scathingly.

"I was a roadie for a rock band."

"Yeah right, so you took the band in the back of your silly lorry!"

"No. I didn't have a *silly* lorry at the time. I drove the tour bus."

"Sorry, but when exactly did you visit Dubrovnik?" Anna asked sternly. It felt like she and Olivia were doubting me.

"Nineteen eighty-nine," I said agitatedly, "and the band was actually quite big and famous. They were called *The Grouse Conspiracy*."

"Course they were, Granddad," Olivia teased me.

"They weren't a big band," Frank growled, "*The Grouse* were a massive band. And I was lucky enough to see them play live in Belfast."

I allowed myself a smug smile — *thank you* — "I believe that would have been in nineteen eighty-six, Frank," I said with relief.

"Absolutely. It was so."

"I'm surprised my uncle didn't try to kill you," Sean muttered.

"That's really not funny, son."

"It wasn't supposed to be."

There was an eerie creak as Olivia shuffled her bottom alongside me. I was aware of the oscillation of the boat, and the sun suddenly felt hotter on my back. It was typical of *The Grouse*, even after all these years the name of the band was still cursed.

Frank sighed heavily and leant towards me. "Tell me," he said, "was it true? You know the story, the legend about John Grouse and the infamous yellow Ferrari?"

"Sadly, yes."

"Go on, then. What's your version?"

"Well . . . I'm not sure if this is the appropriate moment."

"I'm intrigued," Amy said. I wondered if she just wanted to break the tension between the father and son.

"It's a bit raunchy," I warned them, taking a quick look around the boat to gage the reaction of the group.

"Definitely intrigued," Mario said.

Anna shrugged.

"Okay, you asked for this! If you haven't heard other stories about John Grouse, then my advice is not to go looking for them. Even the stuff published tends to be the watered-down version. And this particular incident happened a few hours after the Belfast gig had finished."

"And I was in the pub and nowhere near the band," Frank chuckled.

"Yes, I think I can confirm Frank's alibi," I said. "He has nothing to be ashamed about."

"Who are you trying to kid!" Grace said, squeezing his knee.

"Well, as far as the band were concerned," I continued, "I suppose you could say that they had borrowed or acquired the use of a manor house on the outskirts of the city. It was a place to let their hair down and party. You see, wherever *The Grouse* went on tour, money and fame opened doors, and quite literally on this occasion. When John Grouse got high, he was notorious for going walkabout, and he was snooping around the grounds of this lovely stately home when he discovered a double garage. The garage housed a yellow Ferrari. And John being John, he wanted to drive the car."

"Can't fault the guy's style," Frank interrupted.

"Possibly. Except, it wasn't his car," I said firmly. "Now, there's always girls at these sorts of parties, lots of them. In fact, someone had arranged to transport the entire female staff of a local lap club up to the house. So, John cheekily got a couple of these girls to look for the car keys. The next thing we know, there's a huge bang and the sound of breaking glass. We were astonished to see this yellow Ferrari with two naked girls on the bonnet crashing through the conservatory."

"Oh goodness, but those poor girls," Grace said, "were they injured?"

"Not after delving into John's alternative medicine bag. They simply rolled off the car's mangled bonnet and carried on with the party. Judging by the amount of white powder that was spewed onto the carpet, they probably still can't remember what happened. But the tour had to go on, so we all left for the ferry the next morning whilst the poor manager paid off the owner."

"Brilliant!" Frank said appreciatively. "Good old John Grouse. It was just as I imagined. Do you miss being with the band?"

"Hell no."

"What do you mean?"

"I mean that towards the end, we roadies hated them. When we were touring in Spain, we deliberately took them to a beach that was notorious for a dangerous current and poisonous jellyfish. Sadly, the band survived."

Frank shook his head. "The drugs got them eventually, though."

"Two died from an overdose, and according to reports, John was swept away by a waterfall in Mexico whilst taking a selfie. I don't know or care what happened to Ochie — the band's crazy drummer."

"That's rock and roll," Mario said. "A bit like my boat but without the singing."

I am happy to share these stories, although you can tell by the look in people's eyes that they have no idea what touring with a band is really like. The long and laborious hours of travelling, the grotty sleeping arrangements, the stench of sweat and stale clothes, and the disgusting food that you are forced to endure. Some of the cities we visited were vibrant and amazing, and I saw some incredible architecture, yet others were just ugly and extremely difficult to navigate. Along the way, there were some welcome opportunities for unimaginable sex, but mostly because the band were too wasted to complete the task. Generally, the girls were interested in me for the wrong reasons. I'm not proud of the fact that on many occasions I was letting the girls take advantage of me because they thought that it would get them closer to John. I still don't know what John's greatest downfall was — his irresistible good-looks, natural charm, considerable talent, or his destructive personality. You look at guys like John and Ochie, and you wonder what else they could have done with their lives? Like an avalanche, from the day of their birth they were heading for a messy and bloody crunch when they finally hit the ground. I can't believe that I lasted in the business for eleven years before I escaped. Youth certainly played a part, but it took me far too long to realise that I was becoming damaged by such a manic lifestyle. As for regrets, now I have none. Not a single one. But at the time . . . yes, there were some extremely dark moments.

# CHAPTER EIGHT

"We've had it all today," Amy said, "from destructive winds, to destructive rock stars! But our next stop should be more tranquil. Mario will take us across to the mainland where we will be indulging in part two of our wonderful excursion — the wine tasting."

"Haven't we been doing that for most of the morning?" Sean said.

"Not officially!" Amy said. "The bad news is that Mario won't be joining us. He has to return to Korčula to pick up another party of tourists."

This news was greeted by genuine groans of displeasure. We knew that his departure would buckle the dynamics of the group, a state of harmony that we had been so benignly crafting. I had certainly grown attached to the curious view of his little cabin — his shed.

"I know, I know," Amy continued. "But hopefully you're going to be quickly distracted by the beautiful place that we're heading to. The delightful Orebić is situated on the Pelješac peninsula, and although the spectacular Sveti llija mountain dwarfing the town may look barren and intimidating, even I have managed to conquer its dizzy summit."

"But not whilst drinking Mario's wine," Sean quipped.

"No chance!"

After turning the boat in a circle, we sailed back towards Badija, and then travelled anti-clockwise around the island. Since our arrival in Korčula, I had been captivated by the mountain's dominance of the area. Its presence had teased me from across the bay, and now I felt like an insect scurrying towards its enormous feet.

"Ochie was my favourite member of *The Grouse*," Frank muttered, as if talking to himself. "What a drummer."

"Yes," I agreed politely, "the audience saw him as a great showman, but he could be sadistic at times. He'd deliberately make up stories to cause fallouts amongst the crew. I witnessed a young roadie getting his nose bust because of his blatant lies. Ochie seemed to relish the bloodshed."

"You picked the right guy there, Dad," Sean said prickly.

"In fairness," I added, "I have to admit that Ochie was always good to the fans."

"And the girls, no doubt," Frank gushed.

"Yeah." My voice was barely audible. "But not as much as the other band members." I'd never seen Ochie take much interest in the ladies. Like cattle, the girls were rounded up for John, the band got second pick, and the crew got the spoils. Ochie had grazed elsewhere.

"That's interesting." Sean's eyes bored into me. "And how did you get involved with the band?"

"By complete chance. If my father hadn't owned a van or had a crude knowledge of rigging up lighting, we wouldn't be having this conversation. I was never much help with setting up the sound equipment or acting as a bouncer, but when things took off, John was passionate about loyalty and trust, and I'd been there from the very beginning. Don't get me wrong, I'm not claiming to have been anyone's best mate. Just the opposite. Like any other job, there were good moments and bad ones. Most importantly, it paid the bills."

"Some very good moments, I suspect."

"Yes," I said pensively, "there certainly were."

\*\*\*

My father had earned his living as a landscape gardener. In his spare time, he had two cherished hobbies — looking after the village cricket ground and helping backstage at the local amateur drama group. To me, the cricket ground was just an expansive puddle of morose green grass, and the game itself was slow, cumbersome, and extremely boring. But it is very exciting for a twelve-year-old, sitting in a dark corner of the village hall, to know that your father oversees a vast number of electric leads and flashing lights that are radiating from a strange box in front of you. And he was keen for me to act as his lighting assistant, as it meant that we could spend more time together. Then, seven years later, when an unknown band were trying to put on their first gig in a scruffy building that housed a badminton court, my father's van and his patient training were a great source of help.

Nick, an old schoolfriend, introduced me to John Grouse. It was the early nineteen-eighties, and after some moderate success at school, I was in the final year of a business course at the local college.

Nick worked as a sales representative for Weetabix, and his passions were junk food and music. His company car was a wasteland of empty plastic packages and broken cassette boxes. Like the mess in his car, his musical taste was varied and chaotic, and he often listened to obscure bands and singers. Most of whom I'd never heard of. After a particularly heavy night in a local bar, he had persuaded me to buy a spare ticket for a Chris de Burgh concert in Manchester. The following morning, I awoke with a sore head and considerable dismay at what I'd purchased, yet it would prove to be a decision that would shape my future. The quiet young guy sitting in the backseat of Nick's car on our way to Manchester was John. I remember that he wore tiny round glasses, had floppy hair, and for a reason that I can't recall, I had incorrectly assumed that he was a trainee accountant. It was on the journey home when John came out of his shell. He was especially animated by the moment in the second half of the concert when Chris de Burgh had encouraged his support band to take a break. Then, sitting on a stool placed at the front of the stage, there was just the solo artist, his guitar, and the audience.

I was surprised when we dropped John off at a house on the

outskirts of Leeds and not in our hometown, but Nick explained that John lived in a rented student house that was owned by his brother. Nick had helped to collect the rent one evening, and he'd heard this amazing voice singing in an upstairs room. To my amusement, Nick had been encouraging John to enter some local talent nights and even asked if he could be his manager. 'The talent night is a week on Thursday,' Nick told me as we drove away. 'I'll pick you up at six. And yes, it's going to be awesome! You have to be there.' This would be the first time that I would see John on stage. The last time would be in Berlin on the twelfth of August nineteen ninety-four.

# CHAPTER NINE

The boat docked on an innocuous little jetty on the mainland, and like a bunch of illegal immigrants, we said our flustered thanks and goodbyes to Mario, and scampered onto the hot concrete. He certainly appeared to be in a great hurry to abandon us.

Amy invited us to follow her, and I was reminded of our first meeting earlier that morning when she had led the group around the bay. But now we were cruelly exposed to the sunlight, and on the beach, locals were watching us suspiciously from the shade of the trees. Turning back to the sea, I could see Mario's little boat battling the waves as he turned left towards Korčula.

It seemed as if I had spent my whole life moving on and saying my goodbyes. But all these goodbyes followed the initial and rousing introductions, and I distinctly recalled my strange meeting with Penny in the churchlike, stone porch of her rented house. 'This may sound slightly ridiculous, but you remind me of someone,' I had told her inquisitively.

'Really?' Penny had replied with a devilish smile. 'I didn't know that you were once acquainted with Cleopatra.'

The Irish family led the way up some crumbling steps to a gravel car park. A selection of vehicles were parked lazily alongside an old red boat. One was a large black taxi, and as Amy waved enthusiastically at the driver, I heard the engine starting. "Our carriage awaits," she said, unable to hide her relief. "The taxi will take us the short journey up to the lovely Korta Katarina Winery."

The taxi driver was a wiry looking man with thick grey hair and a matching moustache. His weary sunken eyes looked bored of life, like a pet hamster scrutinising its plastic wheel. Leaving the engine running, he climbed out of his cab and aggressively slid open the rear door, gesturing for Grace and her family to climb inside. Anna needed little encouragement, and then I made room for Olivia. "Daddy used to drive a Ferrari," she declared randomly and smugly as she squeezed past me. "It was wicked."

I shrugged, turning my head towards the window.

There is something bewitching about summertime and the Mediterranean coastline. It's that seductive mixture of heat, dusty roads, and an impeccable blue sea. Korta Katarina Winery was situated on a hill, and its opulent stone buildings enjoyed a commanding view of the Adriatic Sea. We left the vehicle and stood in a huddle, feeling a little uneasy and conspicuous in our beach clothes.

"The property to our left is the magnificent Villa Katarina," Amy told us, her voice almost a whisper. "It's a very fashionable and spacious holiday home with a pebble beach. You can hire it exclusively for up to twenty of your friends and family. There are eight individually styled suites that offer breath taking views."

"Very nice," Grace said, gently rubbing her chin as if she was already selecting nineteen of her friends and family. I wondered if Sean's boyfriend would make the list.

"I don't understand," Anna said. "Is this part of the winery?"

"Yes. The whole complex is owned by an American couple, the Andersons. They came to Croatia in 2001 and helped with the reconstruction of the country following the shocking war in Bosnia-Herzegovina and Croatia."

Amy guided us up to the main entrance of the site. I could see three people dressed in T-shirts and shorts. They were working alongside some noisy machinery. Behind them was a square of beautifully carved arches and narrow pillars. "Daddy would like it here," Olivia said.

"He would," I agreed. "It would be the perfect place to park a red Ferrari."

"Yes. Except, Daddy's car was black."

"That's wicked," I said cheekily. "I once adopted a black cat."

She sighed. "A cat?"

"Yes, but it didn't hang around for long."

"I'm not surprised if you fed it ginger biscuits."

The group shuffled to a stop behind Amy and gawked at the conveyor belt of grapes passing through the machinery. With the sun and exquisite location, the work seemed like a job that had been created in heaven. "This is a treat for us," Amy said, "they're actually processing the grapes today."

We moved inside the building, where Amy was enthusiastically greeted by a young woman in her mid-twenties. I peered into a beautiful room with a stone surround and a long gleaming table in its centre. I could see certificates and photographs standing on an antique wooden cabinet, and bottles of wine were stylishly mounted on the walls. "If you would like to freshen up in the toilets," Amy said, pointing to a dimly lit corridor, "the tour will begin in about fifteen minutes."

I welcomed the opportunity to change out of my T-shirt and was just about to slide my rucksack from my shoulders, when I felt a light tap on my arm.

"I've been thinking," Frank said. "Didn't Ochie have a serious girlfriend at one time?"

"Really?" I said with genuine astonishment.

"Oh yeah," Frank said, like a proud and besotted fan whose bedroom walls were adorned by posters of the band. "She was called Roxy or something. I know this because she went along to some big celebrity wedding with Ochie."

I smiled. "I think you mean 'Rosie'. Yes, that was probably John Taylor's Christmas wedding in the early nineties. The groom was the bass guitarist of Duran Duran and his fiancé was a television presenter."

Olivia gawked at me. I guessed that she had heard of Duran Duran.

"Rosie! Yes, that's the girl," Frank said excitedly. "She was hot. Looked a bit like David Bowie, and she usually dressed like a boy."

"*Exactly like a boy*," I agreed.

"Rosie." Frank skipped down the corridor, a love-struck

teenager cradling his happy memories.

Sean watched his father with curiosity, and then he turned to me. "I promise you that I won't ever tell him the truth," he said, "but just for my own satisfaction, Rosie was a boy, wasn't he?"

I sighed and slowly nodded my head. The world was a vastly different place now, but even without mobile phones and social media, we had never considered Rosie's gender to be a secret. Eighties fashion had often been ambiguous and flamboyant, and Rosie had been lucky to live in a period where men had long hair, wore make-up, and were delighted to be a little different. It was John who had first called him 'Rosie' because of his rosy cheeks and rosy lips. It had suited Ochie to go along with the charade, and he had even encouraged Rosie's more feminine appearance. But when John had begun to refer to Rosie as that 'bloody annoying puffter' a rift had opened between the two of them. It had been an ugly and vindictive conflict that would stretch all the way to the concert in Berlin.

*\*\**

John Grouse's first ever gig was in the *Rose and Crown*, a mundane public house in Otley, West Yorkshire.

I've never seen this fact documented or recorded anywhere, so perhaps during John's countless interviews with journalists and radio presenters, he deliberately chose to forget it. But if Nick is now deceased — I lost touch with him a long time ago — then I'm the only one who can recall this uneventful February evening. I can use the word 'uneventful' with confidence, because the three old drinkers in the bar showed no interest in John at all.

The other act that evening had been more popular with the audience, but this was only because she'd brought her audience with her. Sadly, all seven of them had trooped out of the bar as soon as her fifth and final song had ended. She was a plump-looking girl with a bouquet of pink hair. Her unusual repertoire had included songs by The Clash and The Jam, which sounded peculiar coming from the mouth of a female solo singer. John was undoubtedly the better act, and I was genuinely enthralled by the quality of his voice and his natural talent with the guitar. He began with two John Lennon songs, followed by two that had been sung by Elvis. The fifth song was all his own. It was instantly memorable, and I'd hear *Insufferable Chevin* played many times again, it's addictive melody resonating around vast arenas. John would later explain that he had rashly renamed the song in anger and frustration because the 'old codgers' in the room weren't listening to him. The new name of the song had been taken from the ridge that overlooks the market town. The name stuck.

Nick was far more buoyant about the evening, proclaiming that it had been a great introduction to performing in public, and a month later, the three of us were gathered at the King's Hall in Ilkley for a talent night. We had been encouraged because Nick had discovered that the great Jimi Hendrix had played at one of the town's hotels in ninety sixty-seven. 'I bet his spirit still lingers,' he had hollered elatedly. I had raised an eyebrow, wondering if Chris de Burgh's manager would have said something equally inspiring.

The King's Hall is an old classic theatre with a proper wooden stage. It was a far larger venue than the public house in Otley, and there were at least thirty people eagerly supporting their favourite acts. We felt outgunned, yet hoped that the judges would be impartial to the exuberant cheers from friends, parents, and grandparents. Unfortunately, this might not have been the case. Although John was a credible second, the winner was an eleven-year-old girl. She had wooed the judges and hysterical crowd with *Somewhere Over the Rainbow* from the Wizard of Oz. She was clearly talented, but John took her young age as a personal slur and was seething. To our embarrassment, he couldn't hide his disappointment when she was invited to close the show. During her juvenile rendition of *If I Only Had A Brain,* he shouted an obscenity and angrily kicked over a chair. The audience were rightly furious, and we were told to leave.

This was the first time that I had witnessed the other side of John Grouse. The wannabe rock star and his diverse personalities.

With his guitar slung across his shoulders, he stomped down the pavement and turned into the nearest bar — the lounge of The Midland Hotel. His rage and frustration lasted for a couple of pints of lager until a young woman cheekily asked him to get out his instrument and strum her a tune. He didn't, but his witty and infectious chat appeared to be more than a consolation for her. A second bar brought more drink, and I noticed that John was starting to monopolise our conversation, especially when we had female company. I had assumed that it was his guitar that was attracting their attention, yet even without his trademark spikey blonde hair and designer jeans that would soon abound the teenage magazines, it was already clear that women saw something incredibly special in John.

Nick had promised to limit his drinking to two pints of beer so that he could drive us home, but by the end of the night he had tripled that amount. I regretted getting into his car, but he had assured me that he would use the quiet backroad and follow the river. 'I'll be fine,' he had said optimistically. The March ice might have contributed to the accident, but he spun the car and smashed the rear of the vehicle into a fence. We were unscathed, although a tiddly and comical inspection of the car revealed that the number plate was badly twisted, and the brake lights were broken. With the driver's window wound down and the chill of the night air biting our faces, Nick was using an outstretched arm to make hand signals when the police car spotted us. Looking back now, I think this was the moment that Nick decided he did not fancy the rock 'n' roll lifestyle. He lost his driving licence, and then his job. It would be a few years later before I realised that perhaps it hadn't entirely been Nick's fault, and like the devil, misfortune and destruction followed John Grouse around.

Four months passed before I would see John again.

Due to his miserable circumstances, Nick was reluctantly working in a local supermarket. He told me that the only pleasing part of the job was that it was conveniently close to the bus station, but as he was stuck on the checkout all day, this was a poor consolation. Dreams of managing an artist as successful as

Chris de Burgh were buried under tinned tomatoes and broccoli. One evening, I had borrowed my father's van to take Nick for a drive in the Yorkshire Dales, when he told me that John had joined a small band. They were due to make their debut in a week's time, and as I was now the only legal driver, Nick wondered if I would be interested in giving John a lift. My initial reaction was to decline the offer. Memories of the Ilkley talent night and the long walk home were still fresh in my mind. Nick's car had been abandoned at the roadside and only the inebriated driver had been offered a lift to the police station. Yet, when Nick had explained that the gig would take place on a Saturday evening in a small moor side village called Baildon, the event sounded quite tame. There would be no judges and few pubs to visit, so what could possibly go wrong? After finishing my pint of orange and lemonade, I agreed that I would see John perform for one last time and bring my rock 'n' roll adventure to its conclusion.

The night before the gig, Nick unexpectedly dropped out. He explained that he had to travel down to London for a job interview. It seemed a peculiar time to set off for the city, but as he was struggling with his supermarket job, I simply wished him well. A month later he would relocate to Birmingham, and I've no idea if he ever saw *The Grouse Conspiracy* perform live, or, after their success, even had the appetite to do so.

Thankfully, my father was delighted to take Nick's place and had the foresight to load some portable lighting equipment into the van. When the three of us arrived at the deserted Ian Clough Hall in Baildon, my father was like a true professional, diligently setting up and testing the equipment. John watched him with a mixture of fascination and admiration. At the time, this innocuous moment passed me by, but throughout the entire time we had spent together, John refused to speak about his own parents. After returning from a concert in Lisbon, I remember reading an article in a Sunday newspaper that claimed that in nineteen sixty-four, John's married father had been arrested for attempted rape and abduction. The scandalous part of the story was that the alleged victim was a sixteen-year-old male. However, there was no record of any charges having been brought, and the journalist had concluded that the case had collapsed due to a lack of evidence. I knew better than to bring this to John's attention. He fervently disliked the press.

When the rest of the band arrived in Baildon, my first impression was that I was greeting two lanky hippies and a fat pensioner with greasy hair. It would later transpire that the pensioner was the ex-landlord of the hippies' local public house in Wakefield, who had occasionally filled in when a musician was too drunk to perform or had failed to turn up at his pub. With a cigarette drooping from his mouth, he gruffly announced that he would try his best to convince the audience that he was a reasonable drummer.

The strangely introverted hippies were far more serious about their music, and what was expected of them. Their previous band had broken up when their lead singer and drummer had got a job on a cruise ship, and for tonight's gig, the band had been hastily renamed as: *Two Tall Guys and Friends*.

My father couldn't stifle his laughter.

Although the performance that night wasn't electrifying, the surprisingly large audience — I presumed there weren't many exciting alternatives in a moor side Yorkshire village — had sensed, that like a chrysalis, something magical was emerging. I suppose that if I had to describe their performance, it would be something midway between U2 and Queen. The two tall guys were outstanding musicians, and the poor pensioner gamely tried to hang on to their tails. But John's performance was extraordinary, particularly when he sang two of his own songs.

Later, when we had packed the equipment back into the van and walked up the street to the *Malt Shovel* public house, John was even mobbed by four or five enthusiastic fans. The look on his face was like a dehydrated man stumbling across a waterhole, and the smile grew even bigger as the adulation was mixed with beer. I was happy not to drink any alcohol that evening, which is a rule that I rigorously stuck to when I was working, but I distinctly remember John appreciatively tapping his bottle against my glass of lemonade. 'We're going to need a bigger van,' he said with total conviction, 'and you, my friend, will need to consider getting your Heavy Goods Vehicle Licence.'

# CHAPTER TEN

We were transported by lift to the basement of Korta Katarina Winery. For no discernible reason, I was reminded of the entrance to the lair of a *James Bond* villain.

Apart from Anna, who had just applied a few random smears of make-up, we had all taken the opportunity to change our clothes. Although, I doubted that Anna had noticed this or even cared if she had. She seemed wonderfully untroubled by other people's opinions of her. Her tough Australian character was becoming part of her appeal. She was a *Janice Bond* in the making.

After the hot sun outside, it was a welcome distraction to be greeted by the cool air of the cellar. Our young host, Lana, obviously took great pride in showing guests the winery's underground secrets, and I was astonished at the scale, cleanliness, and the orderly nature of the operation. Everything felt so pristine and important that I felt terrified of touching anything. I had occasionally helped to change the beer barrels at the back of the Social Club, but that was nothing compared to this. The roof and walls were a brilliant pebble white, and I was faced with rows of enormous wooden barrels, gleaming silver pipes, and an immaculately tiled floor. The young woman proceeded to explain how all the parts of the production fitted together and the different roles of the people who were employed there. "I started in the summer of twenty eighteen." She explained. "It was about the time we welcomed our first guests to Villa Katarina."

My mind was drifting, yet I noticed that Olivia was listening intently. This tour of the winery seemed to be one of just a few subjects that interested her. Her mother had told me that she was indifferent to schoolwork, and except for art, she seldom exerted herself. Despite her fascination, I couldn't imagine her doing a job like this in a few years. With her petulant attitude and Daddy's money, I couldn't imagine her working at all. But then, my work history was far from the norm, and life seemed to find a niche for everyone.

Even for people like Gibby.

My respect for *The Grouse* reached rock bottom when they hired a full-time drug dealer and then invited him to join us on tour.

***

Gibby was a regular in one of John's favourite drinking haunts in the centre of Leeds. He was the type of unsavoury character who lingers around the toilets and pesters you for an introduction. This might be something innocuous about football, music, or even the weather, but then he would throw in his grenade: 'Yeah, but we all need some pleasure. Something a little adventurous to help us get through life. And blokes like me, mate, can provide these solutions. *If you know what I mean?*'

He was a man who could get you anything you wanted, no awkward questions asked. And George Gibson or 'Gibby', as most people called him, would argue that it wasn't his fault that there was a sleazy gap in the market. It wasn't his fault that people were desperate to make use of his special and very generous services.

Gibby was of average height, had long shoulder-length hair, lizard green eyes, and he talked incessantly. The words spat out of his mouth like frozen peas, causing his head to make rapid woodpecker movements. You could perhaps describe him as the Yorkshire version of the famous singer, Liam Gallagher, although Gibby had reached his prime long before Oasis had been conceived. He had his faults, but Gibby was at least an original.

I've no idea if Gibby had a contract of employment with *The Grouse* or if he was paid per drugs delivered, but every time we arrived at a new venue, his job was to slink away into the side streets and make the right local connections. I suppose that I should have given John some credit for his business acumen, as Gibby was instructed to work independently from the band. This was to prevent prices being unfairly inflated, and it also meant that the band could be shielded from potentially bad press. 'Gibby pays for himself,' John would often argue. 'His wheeling and dealing saves the band money.' This professional distancing certainly helped when poor Gibby was stabbed to death in an Amsterdam toilet. And, in the crazy and unpredictable world of *The Grouse*, it was the same night that I met Penny. The very first time that I met Penny.

During a busy and exhausting tour of Holland, the band had requested that two rest days should be built into the schedule. I was not surprised that we would be spending this break in Amsterdam, although, I had hoped that the crew might be separated from the band on this occasion. Perhaps the tour manager had negotiated a good deal, or he had decided that it would be safer to have us all under one roof. Like a dysfunctional family, we all stayed at the same hotel.

I was a little apprehensive that John's room was next door to mine, but at least I didn't have to share a twin room with another crew member. The tour manager respected the history that I shared with John, and I appreciated his view that the driver should always get a good night's sleep. But this early night would be on the second evening only, because I had no intention of driving anywhere until we were due to depart the city. It was a holiday for me, too.

When I first set eyes upon Penny, I was in a charming little bar in the red light district. I was waiting patiently for the others. Predictably, John was visiting a girl that he had spotted standing in one of the infamous windows. She was one of three sex workers that he had liked the look of, and it had taken him four circuits before he had finally made up his mind. Gibby was in the window next door — *because any girl would do*. He just didn't care. Ochie had been tempted to visit a window on the other side of the canal, where he'd earlier spotted a skimpily dressed girl that reminded him of Rosie. 'In more ways than one,' Gibby had commented.

The bar was our meeting point. It was in a convenient location, and I could sit at a table above the canal and watch the lights cavorting across the water. I had no interest in visiting one of the intriguing windows — perhaps very intriguing as far as Ochie's 'girl' was concerned. I respected that the girls needed to earn a living, but it was the sleazy clientele that concerned me. People like Gibby. It would be like sharing cutlery with a vagrant.

It was a warm though overcast evening in late June, the canal lounged indolently, its calm surface occasionally blurred by a motorboat returning to its moorings. I decided that I liked Amsterdam.

I had only taken a couple of sips of my ice-cold lager when I heard her voice.

The words of the song were vaguely familiar to me, yet her style was so different that I could not recall the original artist. The song ended to sporadic applause, and I heard some muffled words of gratitude. She teased a few exploratory notes from her keyboard before letting the music flow again. And as the first verse of the next song began, I rose to my feet.

She was elevated on a small stage, a Greek Goddess dressed in brilliant white. I was captivated by her flame red hair and blue eyes. Perhaps I was staring too intently, but she caught my gaze and smiled. The sentiment in her voice intensified. A third song was followed by a fourth.

The three of them arrived together. They stood casually alongside me, making no effort to get a drink. Gibby already looked bored.

'Good, isn't she?' I whispered.

Ochie shrugged. 'Alright, I suppose. But I've had better.'

'Had?' Gibby laughed. 'Like two minutes ago!'

'Not *quite* the same, though,' John baited him. 'I bet some of the notes were a little chunky.'

'*Sssh,*' I warned them. 'Come on, John, show some respect. You must remember what it's like to play in these places.'

'Of course, and I'd certainly consider performing a duet with her.' He sniggered childishly at his crude joke. 'Can't do it right now, though, because Gibby's hideous conquest recommended an interesting coffee shop.'

'Yeah, she did,' Gibby agreed. 'Cos I'm a multitasker, me.'

The three of them laughed, but this joke had the worn hard crust of a tale retold. I imagined them sharing their sordid adventures in the street outside.

I declined their invitation to visit the coffee shop, but no one protested or saw this as a slur. The band was good that way and recognised that we all needed our personal space from time to time. Besides, it was nearly nine o'clock, and we had been exploring the city together since the early afternoon. And not just the quaint canal bars, as John had insisted that we walk to Dam Square and Skinny Bridge. But Gibby had turned his nose up at the Van Gogh Museum, and as John and I had hopped onto a tram, he had persuaded Ochie to come with him to the boisterous Leidseplein.

I had no idea that John had a keen interest in Van Gogh, although I soon discovered that it was not just the paintings that fascinated him — it was the man himself. As we moved from painting to painting, it felt like John was on a desperate quest to prise the truth from the myth. 'Most people think he was crazy because he slashed off his own earlobe,' he explained solemnly, 'but others believe he lost his ear in a fight with fellow artist Paul Gauguin outside a brothel in Southern France. Most importantly, it was Van Gogh who booked himself into a hospital for treatment, which, interestingly, was also known as an asylum. You see how these things can be easily misinterpreted?' I agreed with his logic but pointed out that the poor chap would go on to shoot himself. 'Yes, there is some truth in that. He did sustain a fatal gunshot injury to his abdomen two years later, and supposedly, he revealed on his deathbed that he had shot himself. But did he really mean these words? Was he actually shot by someone else? It was known that he suffered from depression, hallucinations, and seizures due to his unhealthy lifestyle, so if you were bleeding to death, my friend, what tricks would your mind play?'

And a few hours later, John was heading off to get stoned at a coffee shop after visiting a sex worker. That was John.

I found a chair that was positioned closer to the stage. The chair was a one-off. Its high wooden back did not match any other furniture in the bar, which reflected the irony of my current circumstances. Villages and cities are remarkably similar when it comes to strangers drinking alone — it's the norm and no one notices you or cares. There were a dozen people in the bar, although perhaps only a third were listening to the music. This felt like a slur to the artist, and again I was reminded of John's first gig in a small West Yorkshire public house. John's indifference to her talent surprised and annoyed me. There was nothing original in her repertoire, but I enjoyed the manner in which she slowed down each song and made it her own. During the next thirty minutes, she covered songs from artists like *Madonna, Dolly Parton*, *Prince*, and *Everything but the Girl*.

I felt totally at ease when I offered to buy her a drink at the end of her set. I couldn't see any sign of a boyfriend or a family member supporting her, and if she had declined, I would have politely complimented her on her performance and walked out of the bar. This was her working environment. I knew that she would feel safe and relaxed.

'I'm only doing this for fun,' Penny explained after we had completed our introductions. 'Weekends are more popular, but the money is still poor. I can only afford to rent a small space on my friend's floor. It's between an old rocking chair and a rubber plant!'

'At least you can talk to the plant. And in English.'

She smiled. 'Yes. I'm a Northerner.'

'Which part?' I asked.

'Colne in Lancashire.'

'That's crazy. I'm from Yorkshire, just outside Skipton but it's very close to the border. We're practically neighbours.'

'You've lived there all your life?'

'In that area. I grew up nearer to Leeds. You?'

'Left when I was eighteen. Ran away to make my fortune in

Derby! Well, I went to live with a friend. I can't remember if he had a rubber plant. Then I ended up here. It's very laid-back, which suits me fine.'

I had no intention of lying about my reasons for being in Amsterdam and how I earned a living, but equally, I didn't want it to sound like a big deal. I'd like to believe that in all the years that I had worked for *The Grouse* I had never forgotten my simple status. Unlike John, it was quite easy for the band to replace me.

Penny told me that she hadn't noticed that John and Ochie had entered the bar, but she was used to people ignoring her. 'An occupational hazard,' she said. 'Besides, do people comment when you drive well?' Which was a fair point. She was familiar with the band's music, though. 'My God! Sometimes I do my own version of *Insufferable Chevin*.'

'I'm sure that John would have been very complimentary,' I politely assured her, 'especially considering he has also performed in small bars like this one.'

'I guess you have to start somewhere. So where are the band now?'

'Drinking coffee,' I said, choosing my words carefully.

'*Of course*,' she laughed, mimicking the Dutch accent, 'very rock 'n' roll. Do you sing at all?'

'Only when I see a snake.'

'There are plenty in Amsterdam.'

'Yes,' I agreed, 'tonight especially. Do you want to know a secret?'

She smiled. 'I won't tell the rubber plant.'

'Good, because I'm a bit of a fraud when it comes to music and travelling with the band. My heart is with the countryside, and yet I spend so much of my life in huge arenas and vibrant cities.'

'Hey, I'm on your wavelength. When I lived in Derby, I discovered the Peak District, it was only about an hour's drive away. I had this dream of spending my whole life there entertaining the tourists. I did manage to perform on a couple of Saturday nights in Bakewell, but the distance made it impossible to continue. I could hardly travel by bus with all my equipment.'

'I've never visited that part of England. I guess the Lake District is a good alternative if you live in Yorkshire. But the two areas are very similar, there's something wholesome and untarnished in the countryside. I like that wonderful moment when you spot a lamb in a field.'

'I agree,' she said, 'although you have no idea about what the adorable little lamb was up to ten minutes before you arrived. Eating it's mother's poo, I suspect.'

'Perhaps, but I would argue that it doesn't matter. It's what you see and feel at that moment in time. Take a drinks can, for example, and I say this with great compassion, because they constantly roll around the floor of the tour bus. When the can is new, the shape and colours are quite beautiful, but then you crush it with your foot and the beauty and innocence are immediately impaired. And, however hard you try to repair the damage, you cannot ever recreate that moment. It's lost forever.'

She laughed. 'The hours on tour must fly by.'

One drink became three, and she decided that the rented space on her friend's floor was not quite so appealing. 'But a night in a hotel bed sounds very attractive,' she said frankly.

I wasn't shaken by her proposal. We were sitting in a bar in the middle of the red light area. We were young, living for the moment. That moment. Perhaps this was the Amsterdam way. Although, it was ironic that the unspoken things that we both feared, the things that we were so desperate to keep at bay — happy families, mundane careers, stability, children — were all a consequence of the carnal pleasure that we were about to enjoy.

Everything changed when we reached the hotel.

The chairs beyond the reception area were arranged like an impromptu board meeting, and I could see that the tour manager was having a heated discussion with John, Ochie, and two members of the crew. My immediate thought was that there had been an altercation with a photographer or that there was an obsessive fan outside the hotel. I was trying to decide if I should make my presence known or subtly slip Penny up to my room. But the tour manager had already spotted me.

Karl was a rational man who seldom panicked, yet tonight he seemed extremely agitated. Ignoring Penny, he grabbed my arm and pulled me towards the group. Then I discovered the real problem. The cold and harsh facts were that the trip to the coffee shop had not been entirely satisfactory, and Gibby had been despatched to find something more suitable for John's needs. At some point during his negotiations, Gibby had gone to collect a package from a public toilet, and a violent disagreement had left him with a fatal stab wound to his chest. John and Ochie had watched these events unfold from a discreet distance and had then fled when they saw the police arriving. The Two Tall Guys and a minder were believed to be at a nightclub, and a runner had been sent to bring them back to the hotel. This was a damage limitation exercise, although Karl was adamant that as far as the press were concerned, Gibby had no connections to *The Grouse Conspiracy*, and he was merely an old friend of mine from Leeds.

Of course, I challenged this idea. But Karl insisted that I had been walking around the city with Gibby all afternoon, and it was reasonable to believe that this was the first time that John and Ochie had met him. I was still sceptical about this story, and sure enough, eight months later a British journalist would eventually link Gibby to the band, but by this time it was a small article lost in the middle of the newspaper and not headline news.

The worst part of this cover-up was that Karl wanted to take me to the police station to report my 'friend' as missing. On John and Ochie's return to the hotel, Karl had sent a crew member back to the scene of the crime, and as there was so much police activity in the area where Gibby had last been sighted, I would conceivably be concerned about my 'friend'. When I gestured towards Penny, he told me firmly that, as an employee of the band, it was my duty to do this. He assured me that he'd get John to 'distract' Penny in my absence. 'We need to be discreet,' he said, 'make sure that she knows nothing about this.'

It was three hours later before I managed to return to the hotel. The visit to the Dutch authorities wasn't a pleasant experience, and I felt shattered and emotionally drained. Gibby was never my 'friend' but I certainly wished him no harm. I had identified his lifeless and battered body, despite the embarrassment of explaining that I only knew him from a bar in the centre of Leeds, and that he had turned up in Amsterdam unexpectedly. Fortunately, there were no drugs found on his body, so, overlooking their scepticism, the police treated him as a very foolish tourist who was in the wrong place at the wrong time. Thankfully, they also had a good idea of who the perpetrator was, so I never had the uncomfortable feeling of being connected to the crime scene. I genuinely had no idea where poor Gibby had lost his life.

I should have ignored John's door when I reached my hotel room, but I couldn't stop myself from standing listlessly in the corridor. Then, in a trance-like state, I pressed my ear to the cold wooden surface. My tired, woozy head could not dismiss the muffled sounds radiating from behind the door. Some were high-pitched, whilst others were like a drawn-out hum. He either had female company or the television was on. *But why would he be watching Dutch television at this time of the day?*

My worst suspicions were confirmed the next morning when I saw John in the hotel foyer. I felt and looked a mess. My sleep had been fractured by a mushy nightmare of Gibby's long hair, a twisted and deformed face, and a beautiful girl floating above the water of a smoky canal. John showed no reaction to my appearance. 'Thanks for bringing that girl back for me,' he said kindly, as if I'd delivered a large box of chocolates to his room. 'It was appreciated, my friend.'

'You mean Penny?'

He shrugged. 'Yeah, I guess.'

'So she did come up to your room?' I tortured myself.

'That's how it works.'

'But . . . You visited the red light district just a few hours before.'

He laughed. 'Sure did. Made the experience even naughtier.'

'What about Gibby?' I said bitterly. 'Weren't you upset about what had happened to him?'

'Oh yeah. It's tragic. Horrible. But I know he would have

approved. Gibby would have called it multitasking – fucking and grieving.'

*And in that order*, I thought to myself. *Got to get your priorities right, John.*

***

Our small party appreciated observing the wine production process through the various phases. There were occasional gasps, mumblings, and even a few polite questions. Yet, our attentive facial expressions couldn't disguise the real reason that we were here. From the moment that Juliet had shown me the itinerary in England, I knew that the most satisfying part of this visit was going to be the wine tasting.

We took the lift back to the upper level and then eagerly walked down the arched corridor. Perhaps the others had also imagined that the tasting room would be a simple structure with a stone floor, wooden benches and a spittoon, because there was a collective gasp of approval when we entered a majestic dining area. When I saw the number of gleaming glasses meticulously laid out on the table, I realised that even a discreet spit would be frowned upon. This was a room of opulence and refined antiques.

I had been a staunch beer drinker during my twenties and thirties but had eventually learnt that many women like to share a good bottle of wine with their companion. I had grown to appreciate the variety and flavours, and if I was fortunate enough to be invited to the house for a meal, I'd always make the time to choose a good vintage, along with a bottle of port. The two of us would drink the latter on the sofa in the lounge, and it amused me that there might often be a snotty child or two spying on us from the top of the stairs. Penny had been the exception. During our brief time together in England, she had wanted to go out and party, and I remember an adventurous Saturday evening in Leeds city centre. We had visited four quirky bars and a jazz club, drinking nothing but cider from the bottle.

Lana invited us to take a seat, and I was charmed to see that

Amy was the first to take her place at the top of one of the tables. It was as if her duties were over now and she was just one of the gang. I wondered how many times she had been inside this room and the different kind of tourists that she had had to politely spend her day with. I doubted that I would have the patience. There were occasions during my deliveries that even the radio presenters annoyed me. But at least I could call them rude names or switch channels.

I pulled out a splendid wooden chair that was positioned between Anna and Olivia. With their backs to the door, Grace and her family took the three chairs on the opposite side. To our left was a stunning view of the glistening Adriatic Sea, whilst the towering grey mountains eclipsed the side windows. I felt privileged to be here, almost humbled.

An attractive blonde lady arrived with a generous platter of tapas and our first bottle of wine. Holding up the treasured prize, she began to tease us with a detailed description of the ingredients. The secret was slowly revealed. This bottle contained a red — Plavac Mali Reserve — a boisterous flavour of dark fruit and berries. Then, putting us out of our misery, the contents were evenly dispersed between our seven glasses. Later, a white wine would follow — a Pošip — with its delicate bitterness and passionate citrus taste. I settled down into my chair and memories of Amsterdam and *The Grouse Conspiracy* were momentarily forgotten.

# CHAPTER ELEVEN

We were now blessed with the company of two enchanting hosts, Lana and Mia. There were five wines to taste in total and the young women took it in turns to zealously describe the flavours and the locations of Korta Katarina vineyards. Lana explained that after the Andersons had established this property in Orebić, they had begun to acquire small pockets of land in the Dingač and Postup regions of the Pelješac Peninsula. The first vintage of wine was released in 2006. I relaxed into my chair, swilled the wine around my glass, and listened with interest. This was how history should be taught.

The mood was buoyant in the tasting room, and the table had the air and warmth of a family Christmas dinner. It's strange how the mind plays tricks on you, yet for a few moments, I struggled to keep control of my emotions as I was swept back to the slightly awkward Boxing Day meals that I had spent with just my father. I was too young to fully understand what the occasion had meant to him, but the memories of how hard he must have tried to replicate the exciting and manic Christmas Day I had spent with my mother, aunt, and young cousins, were painfully clear.

Olivia's body language was radiating her enjoyment of the wine, the company we shared, and the environment. Suddenly, I was overcome by a strange feeling of gratitude that she had joined me on the trip. Perhaps it was the effect of the alcohol, yet it almost seemed right that she was here and not her mother. *It was meant to be.* I enjoyed being in a relationship with women, but I knew that there would always be times when I needed my own company, needed my own space. Needed my own house. Just like my father, in my adult life I had spent most of my Christmas Days alone. It was a time for parents and their children, and one year, I had even been shunned to allow an ex-husband to return to the family table. The mysteries of Christmas and humanity.

"I assume you live locally, Mia?" Grace's voice banished my thoughts.

"Yes, of course. Korta Katarina is easy for me to walk to, and very lovely in the summer."

Grace smiled warmly. "How convenient. And I bet you enjoy your work?"

"She's probably not allowed to drink the stuff, Mum," Sean quipped.

"No!" Mia said. "I am certainly not drinking today. That would be fun! But I do love working here and living in Orebič. Who wouldn't like it?"

It was Anna who answered this question. I had no idea what she had said to our host, and it was clear that Mia was equally surprised. "You . . . You speak Croatian?" she gasped.

"Yes," Anna replied, flipping effortlessly back to her Australian accent. "I am Croatian. My name is Ana. It's spelt with just one 'n' — A N A."

This bizarre and startling confession was like hearing a thunderclap or a loud rasp on the windowpane. The room was plunged into an eerie and stunned silence, and none of us could quite understand what was going on.

"I'm confused," Amy blustered for the benefit of us all. "I thought you were Australian. You certainly sound Australian."

"I am Australian. I have dual nationality. Sorry, I didn't want to deceive anyone, especially as you're all so lovely. It's just that it's such a wonderful place here and listening to the history of Korta Katrina took me back." She hesitated. "Nineteen ninety-one seems such a long time ago now."

"Nineteen ninety-one?" Mia challenged her.

"Yes. This was the year that my parents fled Dubrovnik."

"The war," Frank mumbled, almost trance like.

"That's right," Ana said quietly. "I was smuggled out of my

grandma's house on the 7<sup>th</sup> December. I was just six years old, and my family had initially thought that it would be safe for me to stay with her in the Old Town. I mean, it's so beautiful, so important to us all."

"But it wasn't safe," Frank said sternly. "The Old Town of Dubrovnik was one of the most dangerous places to be."

Ana slowly nodded her head. "Over two thousand bombs were launched by the Serbo-Montenegrin army. We didn't know which way to run, the bombs seemed to come from everywhere — the sea, the air, and the hills. It was absolutely devastating."

"My God!" Amy said. "We pick up occasional stories about the past, but nothing so personal. It sounds horrendous."

"It was. I can't deny that . . . But hey, I don't want to ruin the party. My life is good and peaceful now, well, except for the sharks and the crocs."

"We have also lived through troubled times in Ireland," Frank said reflectively.

"They know, love," Grace said softly, "they know."

"But they don't know, do they?" He said mournfully. "And just like Ana's tragic past, this is equally important. It's been difficult for our family, too, very difficult at times. You see, my brother was killed during *The Troubles*. It split us right down the middle. Christ, it was painful. Like the blow of an axe." He picked up a piece of pitta bread from his plate and tore it apart. "My brother died whilst trying to plant a roadside bomb . . . but . . . but whatever your views, whatever your motives, there's never an excuse to hurt others." He stared at Ana. "I'm so sorry. There was no excuse to bomb your beautiful city."

"You're right, Dad," Sean whispered. "So right . . . but you did nothing wrong. You've nothing to be ashamed of . . . I know that now. You're a good man. You always have been, always will be."

The family sat with tears streaming down their faces, and I could sense Mia's confusion at the grief that these strangers were seemingly showing for her country. But I too had been brought up with the daily television pictures of the Belfast streets and knew that their minds were a long way from a chilly December day in

Dubrovnik.

"We have one more wine for you to taste," Lana said awkwardly, as she brought a new bottle to the table. "A very special one to welcome back old friends and thank you for your visit to us today."

Amy had spun her body so inelegantly and perilously in her chair that I was concerned she might topple to the floor. "Really? Another one? How intriguing," she said, clearly a little flustered by the revelations of the last few minutes. I had the feeling that today's visit to the winery was not one of her typical days at the office. It was becoming an interesting day for the entire group.

Cradling the handsome black bottle in both hands, Lana smiled deviously. "This wine originates from the infamous Pošip grape of Dalmatia and is a premium white sparkling wine. Any ideas about this one, Amy?"

"Um . . . a few, but I'll let you make the revelation."

"It's our Korta Katarina Sabion Brut."

"Oh wow! What a fabulous way to finish the tour!"

The bottle might have contained liquid gold by the stunned manner in which we watched Lana pour the elegant wine into our glistening glasses. The inside of my head felt gravity free — a mushy, cosy, woozy tapestry of alcohol and flavours. And Olivia was sitting quietly besides me, listening to these peculiar adult conversations in a similar state of stupor.

I felt a niggling and perhaps irrational guilt that I should have been more responsible for her drinking, but she was nearly eighteen, and there hadn't been time to discuss the visit to Korta Katarina with Juliet. I decided that it would be a learning curve for her, and if she felt hungover in the morning, she could always ring Daddy for some sympathy. Yet strangely, part of me didn't want that to happen. I hoped that we could sit by the pool and suffer together.

\*\*\*

No one had offered me any sympathy when I had discovered the truth about Penny. Although, sympathy wasn't something that I sought out. My father was dead, I did not gossip about my personal life in the Social Club, and many years had passed since I had walked away from *The Grouse*. It still alarms me that it wasn't until our third meeting that I finally realised that I had met Penny before. The events in Amsterdam had happened some twenty-eight years ago, but it was inevitable that my past would come up in our conversations eventually. She knew how I was earning a living now because she had hired me to transport some of her furniture in my lorry. Like all developing relationships, we had been surfing the top of a wave, but then, without any warning, a deep chasm of water lay beneath us. Penny had been reluctant to open up and it was only through questioning her about the silver-framed photographs on display that I learned she had an ex-husband and a son. The son was in his mid-twenties and living in New Zealand. The ex-husband had served in the military and was now based in Dubai. Conversation closed.

Later, the subject of music had been raised. She had recently visited Ambleside in the Lake District with an old school friend, and they'd heard this wonderful young singer performing in a quaint and cosy bar. Penny had said that his performance had felt so intimate that it took her back to a special time in her life. She asked me if I'd be interested in taking a train into Leeds with her on Saturday evening. She'd been told about a place called *The Four of Clubs*, an underground bar offering live jazz, blues, and soul music. 'That will take me back to my youth, too,' I told her enthusiastically. 'You see, I used to be a crew member for *The Grouse Conspiracy*.'

'I once met John Grouse,' she said without any trace of reverence. 'He was on tour in Holland.'

'Amsterdam,' I had mumbled with a debilitating numbness, because in that instance everything had come hurtling back to me. Her dyed red hair, her beautiful music, the canal side bar in the red light district, and finally, Gibby's tragic murder. 'I was right, we have met before,' my words seemed to echo, resonating from wall to wall of her small living room. 'You were singing in a bar in

Amsterdam.'

Then, after her initial surprise, she had said dourly. 'You deserted me that night. Just vanished into thin air.'

'Didn't John explain?' I asked, although I knew he'd been warned by the tour manager not to tell her the truth.

She shrugged. 'I got the impression that you were employed to deliver girls to John. I also remember that he could be very persuasive, yet equally charming. Anyway, that's how I recall things.' Again, conversation closed. Like the end of a song in a bar next to a canal, the sound of her voice slowly drifting away, slowly suffocating. A body on a slab in a morgue. But neither of us really wanted to revisit that night.

At first, I had told myself that her brief acquaintance with John didn't matter. It was a long time ago, and it was my fault that I had left her in such a vulnerable position. I should have told her that I had some urgent business to attend to, told her to leave the hotel. *Did I really think that I would return from the mortuary and find her chatting amicably with the band in the hotel foyer?*

We did visit Leeds and *The Four of Clubs*. It was one of the most wonderful nights of my life — that illicit taste of cider from the bottle, the hum and frenzy of the city bars, the thrill of live music — until the taxi drew up outside her house. It was after two o'clock in the morning. Penny had fallen asleep in the back of the car, and there, sitting smugly between us, was John's ghost. I knew that it was the effect of the alcohol, yet I couldn't get him to leave. The taxi came to a gentle halt, rocking Penny's head until her eyes opened sleepily. She stared at me and pulled a childish face, before gently rubbing a finger across her lips. It was very clear that she wanted me to stay with her. 'Go ahead, my friend,' John had whispered, 'it's your turn now.' *But is it, John? Is it really my turn?* 'Sure, and it should be easy for you, remember, I'd already had one girl that day. What is it that Gibby called it after we'd visited those sex workers? Ah yes, multitasking.' *But what about the drinks can, John? You remember how they used to roll around the floor of the tour bus. You crush the can with your foot and its beautiful shape is spoiled forever. And what did you do, John? You took the can from me and crushed it. You crushed it with your foot.*

I had made a feeble effort to kiss her on the cheek, before hastily turning away. I didn't say a single word. I was incapable. I left her standing on her doorstep, my head burning with the debilitating thought that for the second time she was feeling hurt and rejected. And that was the end of our acquaintance. There was nothing more. I wasn't offered another opportunity.

*\*\*\**

"I'm sure you'll agree that our hosts have been fantastic," Amy said, making an unsuccessful attempt to push herself up from the table. Her statement and lack of coordination were saluted with laughter, cheers, and a round of applause. "And if you are capable," she laughed at herself, "you are very welcome to follow Mia to the shop and purchase your favourite wine. But I know what you're about to say, so I'll ask the girls to provide a quick recap on what we've had the enormous good fortune to taste today."

Like a well-rehearsed sketch, Lana and Mia produced the empty bottles and held them up in the order in which we had devoured the wine.

"What do you think we should buy for your mother?" I asked Olivia.

"I think she'd like a number two," she said and burst out laughing.

"Okay," I agreed, "that sounds perfectly reasonable. The white it is." I strained my eyes to make a note of the name on the label. "I don't know about you, but as far as I can recall, they're all as good as each other."

"Yep," she slurred, "that's about how I recall it. Oh, and how's your back?"

"My back?"

"After your fight with those naughty ants."

I stared at her a moment. "Good. Yes, not bad at all. Thank you for asking."

She nodded. "My pleasure."

I watched her take a photograph of the debris of empty glasses, then, for a final time, I turned to gaze out of the window at the majestic turquoise sea that lay beyond. I thought of John Grouse standing at the edge of the Mexican waterfall that would shortly claim his life. But even without the horrific threat of an imminent death, there are some views that you know you will never see again.

# CHAPTER TWELVE

"We've got about thirty minutes before we need to return to Korčula," Amy said, after finally hauling her svelte body onto her feet. "But after you've bought your gifts, there is a final treat for you all — a speedboat ride home!"

"My poor abused head won't take that," Grace said, "I'll have to swim back."

"To Northern Ireland or Korčula?" Sean teased her.

Frank flicked his thumbnail against his glass and then appeared to gasp in amazement at the high-pitched sound it made. "Listen up! It's not the final treat," he insisted. "You're all invited to visit my bar in Korčula town. And the first round is on me!"

"Your pub, Frank?" Amy teased him. "I didn't know you owned a pub in Croatia. But it is very kind of you. My husband is going to come and meet me, although I can let him know where I am."

There was no taxi to take us back to the harbour, although Amy promised that the walk back down the hill was far less arduous. Perhaps the only issue was the heat of the sun, but no one complained.

I was amused and delighted to see that Olivia was talking to Sean. Her posture and body language had altered considerably from this morning. There was now a grown up and elegant rhythm in her steps. I walked behind Amy and Ana, discreetly listening to their conversation. "You could have told Mario about your upbringing in Dubrovnik," Amy said, "he would have been delighted to welcome you back to Croatia."

"Nah," Ana said cagily. "I don't know, but sometimes it feels like I ran away. Besides, Croatians tend not to talk about the past. I certainly felt that with Mario when Frank raised the subject this morning. But you're very welcome to pass on my regards the next time you see him."

"I will, and it seems that it's not just Croatians who are struggling to get to grips with their dark history. It's been an unusual day." She abruptly ended their conversation, and I realised that it was because Frank had stepped into the road and was waiting for us to catchup with him.

"I get the impression that Ochie wasn't your favourite band member?" he said to me mischievously.

I shook my head and walked alongside him. "Probably not. But I can't deny there were some days when he amused me. The problem with Ochie was that he wanted people to see him as an enigma. He weirdly described himself as part Mongolian, part Himalayan, and quite a bit English. The English claim was his most credible, because after scouring the Northern music venues for drumming talent, John finally discovered him in Bradford. I didn't understand the Himalayan part until he developed an unhealthy obsession with climbing Everest. He eventually tried it, and the experience very nearly killed him."

"Yeah, that was a crazy idea," Frank laughed. "Totally threw me."

"People like us wouldn't be allowed to attempt such a ridiculous challenge, but if you have fame and money, it seems almost anything is possible. Fortunately, he only managed to get about a third of the way up the mountain before he collapsed. Any higher and he could have risked the lives of his Sherpas and climbing instructors. He was a big bloke. Must have weighed about eighteen stone. So, I've no idea how anyone could have carried him back down. As it was, the band were forced to take an extended break whilst he recovered, and for John, it meant missing out on the opportunity of breaking America. Sadly, *The Grouse* would never get to play there."

"Shame," Frank agreed. "The Yanks would have loved them."

"I agree. It worked out well for me, as I had the time to explore my future options. I did some research into what it would take to set up a delivery business and even did some driving work in a rented van. When the day came when I'd had enough of the band, I had the confidence to buy a second-hand lorry and walk away completely."

"Walk away? Not sure about that, but a lorry is better than building ships."

"That's your trade?"

"Not anymore. The actual ship building finished many years ago, although the yard still constructs those massive floating structures for the gas and oil industry. Until my retirement, I was involved with repairs and refits. Bloody hard work, but I do miss the banter."

"You will have enjoyed Mario's boat trip, then?"

He grunted. "Yes, today was special."

The wind blustered into our faces, goading the dust into a rebellion. I covered my eyes with one hand and fumbled for my sunglasses with the other. The magnificent sea stretched before me, its white and blue coating edgy and cantankerous, taunting me to make the crossing back to Korčula.

It seemed to be a strange moment to board a speedboat.

"You must have made some money from *The Grouse*," Frank cheekily extended our conversation.

"I can't complain," I said. "John was very generous at times, and I bought a house without having to get a mortgage. My legacy with *The Grouse* is a quaint two-bedroom cottage, but I still have to work to pay the bills."

"Yeah, but you were there. I wish I'd been part of something like that."

I half nodded and then half shook my head. It was difficult to explain, but I hadn't wanted any association with the band on that disturbing night in Berlin. "I'm sure there will be a time when I'm slurping a cup of tea in a care home and everything about my past will feel joyous and rosy."

Frank laughed. "Sounds like you're referring to Ochie's girlfriend again!"

"No, I'm definitely talking about a very different kind of rosy."

"Suit yourself."

I'm not sure what I was expecting to find at the harbour, but the speedboat looked as intimidating as the waves. It was the shape of a spear, and apart from a tiny cabin for the lucky driver, the passenger seats were open and vulnerable to the elements. Olivia was less concerned, and she followed Ana towards a triangle of seats at the bow of the boat. Relieved to see that Ana had chosen the intimidating seat at the front, I squeezed my body into the next space beside Olivia.

During the entire journey, I never saw the driver of the boat or found out his name. I will just remember him for an insane fifteen minutes of terrifying elevations, tumbles, and bumps. We were like a clumsy swan trying desperately to get airborne, and Olivia laughed and cheered all the way. "Don't tell me your father owns a speedboat?" I shouted through the spray.

"No, but I wish he did!"

Ana's exuberance also intrigued me. She treated the speedboat like a roller-coaster ride, her arms held high to the sky. It was as if she had cast off the heavy cloak of the past and was now celebrating her life and survival. My mind drifted back to the grand dining table of Korta Katrina, and I remembered Frank's guilt and sorrow. *When soldiers or terrorists haughtily flick their explosives onto cities and towns, do they ever think about the futures they are destroying and depriving? Truly, wonderful and beautiful moments like these.*

# CHAPTER THIRTEEN

Like a schoolmaster, Frank was eager to climb onto the jetty first to herd us to his favourite bar.

"Are you okay with another drink?" I whispered to Olivia.

"Lightweight!" she teased me. "And I thought you were an old rocker?"

"I was going to send you back to the hotel with a message," I explained, "but I can always text your mother."

"Send me back?" she asked mournfully. "Don't you want me to come with you to this bar?"

"Yes, very much so. I think we're in this together."

"We sure are, Cowboy."

I didn't understand her comment, but it made me smile.

"Anyway," she added, "now we'll both need to use the toilet."

"Sure will." *Cowgirl.*

*Frank's Bar,* as it would be affectionately named for the rest of our holiday, was on the far side of Korčula's Old Town. Its row of inviting tables and chairs nestled in the shadows of the medieval walls, with the spectacular Sveti llija mountain dominating the horizon.

"We come here most evenings," Grace explained. "Our delightful accommodation is just a short walk away."

"Dad calls it 'early doors'," Sean said, rising his eyebrows.

Frank brazenly scraped a metal table across the cobbles as he constructed a little den where we could sit and chat. "Who will join me in a large cold beer?" he cried exuberantly.

"Or alternatively, a refreshing cocktail?" Sean counteracted.

"I'm for the huge beer," Ana said unsurprisingly.

I nodded my agreement.

Sean picked up a drinks menu and beckoned the girls to gather around him. He then held court, excitedly describing the various concoctions he had sampled since his arrival. It dawned on my why Frank had been so keen to bring us here. He was missing his shipyard mates who would eagerly guzzle their beers alongside him, tell smutty jokes, and never even think of ordering a cocktail. I had the feeling that during these 'early doors' gatherings in Belfast, Frank would have been keen to change the subject if the discussion was about their offspring.

The waiter came over and Frank couldn't conceal his pleasure when the young Croatian warmly shook his hand. Frank ordered his 'usual' — a large Ožujsko beer — with two additions, and then sighed heavily when Sean requested more decision time for his subgroup. The waiter shrugged and told us that he would serve the beers and then take the cocktail order. "Same problem every night," Frank said wearily.

There's nothing quite like a cold beer after a barrage of wine. It was like being greeted by an old friend, the selfless pleasure of a gentle shoulder nudge. Frank smiled when he read the satisfaction on my face and then swung his body towards Ana. "Do you remember anything about that December night?" he asked bluntly.

Ana seemed a little confused. Her beer hovering below her lips.

"The siege of Dubrovnik?" he persisted.

"Sorry, I was just . . ." she said hesitantly. "You know, if you'd asked me that question a month ago, I wouldn't have been able to answer you. I didn't know how or where to begin. It wasn't something I ever wanted to revisit. But since my return, yes, *oh God yes*. I might have been a child at the time, but I could sense the tension leading up to the attack. And then, after I was smuggled out of Dubrovnik's Old Town, it took a good month to escape the country."

"And your parents weren't with you?"

"No. I was staying with my Grandma that particular night. It was something that I enjoyed doing. We were very close."

"Did you have family in Australia?" I asked her more gently.

"Yes, an aunt. My mother has always been close to her sister, so it seemed the right time to go out to Australia. My father joined us much later, but my Grandma refused to leave. She died before I had chance to see her again."

"But not because of the war," Frank said coldly.

I squirmed. It felt like the poor woman was being interrogated.

"No, although thirteen civilians did lose their lives on the 6th December," Ana said, her voice calm and methodical. "A lot of the bombardment was concentrated on Stradun, which is the central promenade of Dubrovnik's Old Town." She turned to face me. "I know it was a long time ago, but did you visit the promenade during the band's tour?"

I shook my head. "Sadly, my only memory is walking the spectacular old walls. I didn't carry a camera, and, in those days, there were obviously no camera phones. But last Saturday afternoon, Olivia managed to photograph them through the window of the minibus after we had left Dubrovnik airport. There was an impressive view from the main road."

"The walls are amazing, aren't they? You'll have seen what I was talking about during your visit. An obscene amount of missiles and mortar shells were thrown at us. But this wasn't the first assault that we endured. In mid-November, the boats in the harbour were attacked. There was a short ceasefire after this, but it didn't last. I remember a period of anger and confusion. You pick it up from your parents, because it's just too big a thing for them to hide. Besides, we lost our electricity supply and fresh water."

"And this is the first time you've returned?" I asked.

"Yes, it is. My father said that I needed time to heal. Time to forget the nightmares. Although, maybe the longer you stay away, the worse things become. There's a war museum in the fortress at the top of Mount Srđ. You can reach it by cable car. The views are magnificent. I tell you, that was a big moment for me. I can still feel it now. My mother warned me not to visit the museum, but I felt I had to. I stayed there for about three hours. The use of television news coverage of the siege is very clever as it makes it so visual, so realistic, and so truthful to my own memories. What do you call it? Facing up to the past and cleansing the mind. They've repaired the damage very well, and I bet most of the tourists have absolutely no idea about the destruction caused."

"I like that," Frank said. *"Cleansing the mind."* He rubbed his chin as if storing the words beneath his beard. "But Dubrovnik is all about those Game of Thrones tours now. People can't separate fact from fiction."

Ana took a gulp of beer. "I've never seen the television series, never really fancied it, but yeah, the current residents of Dubrovnik are certainly exploiting it. There are walking tours and merchandise everywhere. In twenty years' time, it will be all that people remember. Thank God for Korčula. This is the sort of memory that I need to take back to Australia."

"I'll drink to that," Frank agreed.

The waiter was walking towards our den with a tray of cocktails, his dark brown eyes staring wistfully at Olivia. He announced his arrival with a graceful bow and carefully unloaded the glasses onto the table.

"What have you got there?" I asked Olivia.

"I don't know!" She gushed. "But Sean said that I'd like it."

"Well, he was right about the snorkelling."

She nodded her head and took a tentative sip. "Oh wow! I like. *I really like.*"

I laughed and gazed up at the imposing dome of medieval wall that stretched above me, the glow of red roofs glistening above the sandstone. Despite Ana's disturbing account of her past, I'd never felt such peace.

"What do you think happened to Ochie?" Frank's voice rumbled.

I slipped back into my chair and stared at him. "I have no idea."

"Come on!" he challenged me. "You must have an inkling."

"Honestly, I really don't know. I have been well out of the band for some time, and I've lost all contact with the support crew. We were never particularly close. It's strange, but when you do try and find out anything about him, he's not described as 'missing' but 'unfound' — like an old Pharaoh's tomb. There were reports a few years ago that he had been seen in Vietnam, but how many people would actually recognise an old forgotten rock star in his late fifties?"

"That's not old!"

"It is in the music industry. Especially, if the band is quite literally dead and dysfunctional. There's definitely no chance of a reunion."

"I hope that he's sitting on a beach somewhere," Frank mused.

"Yes," I said, but the disturbing thought in my head was *who the hell with?*

***

The manner of John's death was incredulous considering his lifestyle. The notion of a wild and rebellious rock star dying whilst taking a selfie at a tourist attraction was farcical. He wasn't even naked. Although at least he had the satisfaction of dying in the company of a gorgeous young lady — the only witness. Some reports said that the time of his death had been at sunrise. So perhaps John had finally experienced some romance seeping through his weary veins. Or maybe he was pushed.

More fittingly, but equally tragically, the Two Tall Guys had died a couple of years before John. They had overdosed within three months of each other. The first death was accidental, but the second was a suspected suicide.

The Two Tall Guys were without doubt the strangest and most aloof couple that I'd ever met. Even the press gave up on them, instead focusing their attention on John and Ochie. Not that this ever seemed to concern them. They appeared to have a telepathic understanding of each other, like robotic twins built in a laboratory. Yet, there was never a physical love attached to their relationship, no threesomes with girls or evidence of anything deviant. Women were serviced and despatched in the same clinical manner in which John dealt with the opposite sex. Some suggested it was because of their fascination with heroin —

the silent smiling queen that controlled their lives — but I had met them from the very start, and the drugs had not changed their personalities.

The Two Tall Guys just wanted to live inside their own unique bubble, and any conversation with the outside world was met with a long and drawn out stare. You always got the feeling that you were annoying them. To me, they were like an old book on a dusty shelf, a book that I'd never opened or knew anything about. I certainly never understood how the band's relationship worked in the recording studio or on stage. They simply communicated with John and Ochie through their music. And John never had a bad word to say about them. 'They're like the birds in my back garden,' he once told me. 'I will never tire of them, and I totally respect what they do. But I know if I ever try and get too close, they'll fly away.'

John was different. If the Two Tall Guys were the birds, he was the badger. A creature of elegance, fascination, and allure.

My relationship with John was like a plant. Whilst his life blossomed above the surface, I was that ragged piece of turf where the roots take anchor.

Our conversation usually felt stilted, contrived, before reluctantly tumbling into a common groove that begrudgingly accepted that we were both tormented souls. Then we almost became entwined, the same. Bonded with guilt about this strange adventure that had paid the bills and crafted our lives. The subject was never raised, never discussed, but we knew that we'd make lousy fathers. And now John was dead, his family tree had been pruned, terminated, the wooden stump brittle and exposed.

I remember crying when I heard that he had died.

I'm not usually the sentimental type, so it was completely out of character. It was a Tuesday evening, and the only time when I broke my no alcohol rule before driving the next morning. I still don't know if those tears were a sign of my relief or nostalgia — perhaps a longing for a renaissance with something extraordinary that had been lost in time. I locked the doors, shut the curtains, pulled out a beer from the fridge and fumbled through my music collection for anything that *The Grouse Conspiracy* had recorded. I'd not heard any of their music since that disturbing concert in Berlin. One beer had followed another, as I listened to all their albums. And every song, every riff, brought back memories of my relationship with John. I hadn't been entirely truthful to Frank. John was never my best friend, yet for a good few years, I was certainly his. And, perhaps by walking away from the band, I had abandoned him.

***

I was distracted by Grace's squeal of excitement and glanced sideways to see a man holding the hand of a pretty little blonde girl. "Here are Emma and Michael," Amy said proudly.

"So cute," Olivia said tipsily, almost managing to point at the pigtails in Emma's hair.

"Sorry, which one is Michael?" Sean quipped, before fussing around for another couple of chairs. The weary waiter was forced to make his fourth trip to our den, although, once again, his gaze was firmly set on Olivia.

Michael was in his mid-thirties, a small and muscular man with the build of a fell runner. I wondered if he rose at six o'clock every morning, put on a pair of shorts, and followed a fitness regime in front of the television. He told us that he ran the business alongside Amy, and it would be his turn to take out another group of tourists in the morning. He joked that it would be easier than looking after Emma.

"Are you sure about that?" Grace challenged him. "You didn't have to put up with us lot!"

"Well, Amy must have done something right today," Michael said, "because no one has ever invited me for a drink after the tour."

"What can I say," Amy said bashfully.

Frank raised his empty glass. "I know what we can say — *thank you*."

I offered to buy the next round of drinks, but Amy declined. "I know that it's rude of me to go," she explained, clumsily finishing her drink, "but we have to go and do the weekly shop." It seemed to be a bizarre thing to say considering the beautiful location we were in and the wonderful day we had spent together, yet for her family, this was a job. This was their home.

Ana also took the opportunity to depart, and you could almost feel a tremor resonating around the den as we realised that this extraordinary day in our lives was drawing to a close. And more uncomfortably, we would never meet again.

Age makes you more aware of moments like these, and I decided that I should be grateful for those mind-numbing statistics that had somehow put us in the same place together at the exact same time. Implausible probabilities that had briefly allowed us to share a small part of our lives. And, as human beings do, we politely said our goodbyes in the kindly and respectful manner of old mates who *would* meet up again the following week.

Frank did not take any persuading to have a second beer, although Grace's distorted mouth and scrunched up nose made it obvious that she was keen to return to their accommodation. She reluctantly agreed to have a tonic water. Sean underplayed his desire to have another cocktail and suggested to Olivia that perhaps they should have 'one for the road'.

"Is the road thirsty?" She teased him.

When the waiter arrived with our drinks, Olivia asked him to take a group photograph. He was delighted to oblige, and standing close to her side, cheekily made her demonstrate which buttons he should press. By the manner in which their touching fingers lingered as he returned her phone, I knew that this wouldn't be the last time that we visited *Frank's Bar*.

"Come on, tell me one final great rock 'n' roll story," Frank said, as the waiter reluctantly went back to the inside seating area.

"Haven't you heard enough about *The Grouse?*"

"No," he said indignantly. "Anyway, what else do you want to talk about? And don't say bloody golf!"

"No chance there. Unless . . . Olivia?"

"*I don't play golf!*"

"That's true. Okay, let me think," I said. "Right, got one. But this sad tale was certainly a harsh lesson for me, and there was nothing glamourous about either what we did nor the location. It happened in John Grouse's hometown of Leeds."

"No complaints from me," Frank said rubbing his hands.

I couldn't help but smile. It was like throwing treats to a puppy. "We'd just returned from London, and the band were euphoric because it had been the first time they'd rocked the capital. I remember listening to the excited banter as I drove the bus, and it was thoroughly deserved. The gigs they'd played were a great success. Additionally, the band had recently signed a promising recording contract, and a local businessman and keen sponsor had arranged a homecoming — a private party for the band at his impressive property in the city's suburbs. It was a place called Moortown, if you're interested in the detail."

"I've been there," Olivia said proudly.

"Posh, isn't it?"

"Well, the places I've been to."

"Just let rip, girl!" Sean said. "Tell him straight."

"Fair enough," I laughed. "Having driven the band to their first ever gig in a tiny village hall, I was very much a part of things in those days, and it was taken for granted that I would be fully involved with the celebrations. After we had parked the bus, the night began as a pub crawl around the city, and then stretched to a nightclub where we were introduced to some of the Leeds United football team — not that this particularly excited the members of the band."

"Me neither," Frank said. "Liverpool is my team."

"Stevenage Town," Sean said randomly.

Frank howled with laughter.

"Anyway," I continued, "about one o'clock in the morning, we were shuttled by taxis to the private venue. We had been well looked after in the city. The supply of champagne, beer, and shots were seemingly endless, and it had been a fun night. This had been perhaps the first time I had witnessed the adulation for the band,

and it was clear they were quickly becoming celebrities. Then things got really interesting. John wasn't impressed with the lack of female presence at the private party — who were mainly middle-aged friends of the host — although we were compensated in other ways." I lowered my voice. "There was a huge stash of drugs."

Frank grinned evilly and took a greedy slurp of beer.

"Yes, exactly. In the spacious and impressive modern kitchen, we discovered a line of cocaine that stretched from one end of the work surface to the other. The line was like a train journey across the Sahara Desert and someone had ingeniously built a chicane to bypass the toaster and kettle. Now, for once, I had no driving duties lined-up for the next day, so I made a reckless decision to indulge. Olivia, I beg you, please don't ever tell your mother."

"You'd better be nice to me, then," she said prudishly, although the sly grin on her face made it quite clear that she was delighted to be part of this deviant secret. "Especially, when we're visiting bars like this one."

"You'll go far," Sean said admiringly.

"And I'll be bankrupt," I said, raising my hands in mock protest. "Anyway, back to that naughty white stuff in the kitchen. John started at one end of the line, and I began at the other, but thankfully, we didn't meet in the middle! Instead, we crawled slowly out of the backdoor and sprawled out on the lawn. Lying on our backs, we must have stared at the stars for at least an hour or so, which is ironic, because over the years I discovered that rock stars believe they have a connection with the universe and the Gods! Sorry, I digress. Perhaps rudely, John and I decided that we wouldn't return to the party, but instead, walk down the country lanes to the main road and flag down a passing taxi. It was about four o'clock in the morning by now and John had asked if he could crash at my place. There were many times when he didn't care for his own company. A few hours earlier, getting home would have been a very simple thing to do. I'd grown up quite close to this area, but after our indulgence, it now seemed like someone had rewritten the road signs in Japanese. They made absolutely no sense to either of us and despite the obvious lights of the city centre, we had no idea which direction we needed to take. Eventually, after walking for hours, we got lucky. Despite being lost in a dimly lit backstreet, a taxi pulled up and the driver bravely wound down his window. However, when he asked me the straightforward question of where he needed to take us, I couldn't for the life of me remember where I lived. Understandably, he accelerated away. It was daylight when I awoke, and once again, I discovered that we were sprawled out on a garden lawn. I recall having a niggling feeling that we were not at the venue of last night's party. And I was right. But despite our long and reckless efforts to reach my home, we were just two doors down from the businessman's house and still stuck in bloody Moortown!"

"That's a funny story," Frank said appreciatively. "Very good."

"Why am I not surprised to hear you say that, Frank?" said Grace. "Ah yes, just substitute the cocaine for Guinness and you could have been in it — *and hundreds of times!*"

"Well, I can assure you," I said, lifting my glass, "this would be the last time that I ever indulged in naughty substances with the infamous John Grouse."

***

The morning of the Berlin concert gave me some of the happiest moments that I had ever spent with John. I had no idea at the time that it would also prove to be the last morning I would share his company.

With his facial features crudely and comically disguised beneath a tacky tourist cap, he suggested we should do some sightseeing. During breakfast, he had made a long list of the places we should visit, although we only had time to see three historical places — the Brandenburg Gate, the Reichstag building, and the Berlin Wall Memorial. They were probably the easiest places to reach from the hotel. It was a pleasure to be in John's company, and I wasn't sorry that the rest of the band or crew had not been invited. By this point, John had more of a business relationship with the Two Tall Guys, and Ochie was becoming an irritant. Every time we went on tour, I was amazed at how all these issues could be forgotten from the moment that the band walked on stage. Their music was like a vice, a state of hypnosis, where everything else was overlooked. It gripped their upper torsos, whilst their legs thrashed and rebelled wildly below.

Seven years had passed since the United States President Ronald Regan's prestigious and well documented visit to Berlin, and John's enthusiasm and knowledge of the city's history had surprised me. I had no idea that the design of the Brandenburg Gate was inspired by the Propylaea, the gateway to the Acropolis in Athens. 'But we rocked Athens,' John had teased me. 'I dragged you up the hill to show you the damn thing!' It had been Gibby who had begrudgingly trekked up the hill with him that hot afternoon, but I gave John his moment.

The Berlin Wall Memorial was a sobering experience. 'Such a crazy and terrifying idea,' John had said gravely. 'One hundred and fifty-five kilometres, dissecting fifty-five streets, almost impregnable, and yet, I bet Ochie would still have been on my bloody side of the bricks!' I watched him press his hand against the dull stained concrete. 'It's the same stuff the world over, isn't it? Sand, mortar, gravel, and water, except this small line of concrete means so much more.'

'Just like people,' I said. 'We have queens, presidents, pop stars, and then there are the roadies.'

'But we are all part of the cement, my friend. Some are just hidden behind the crumbling surface, like the nameless people who made this piece of wall. Whatever happened to them?' He took his hand away and slowly lifted his chin, his eyes tracing the cracks and crannies to the bulbous peak. 'You know, sometimes I feel that we're the guilty generation — the youngsters who supposedly mope around and play music instead of going off to war. Sure, there are those who were born in the nineteen-forties who also missed those long years of carnage, but when they were our age the world was still in that period of relief and reflection. But now, as those brutal memories begin to fade, we're the generation who will always have to be thankful.'

'We are thankful,' I said, 'but maybe there's a new song that needs to be written to represent our feelings?'

He shook his head. 'My friend, that would just make us the whinging and ungrateful generation. I don't wish to put a greater burden on our shoulders, so we'll just have to live with the stigma.'

Later, when we started setting up at the stadium, the rehearsal and sound checks went smoothly without any hiccups, and these positive vibes were carried on into the concert itself. Maybe it wasn't *The Grouse's* best ever gig, but it was certainly in their top five. Berlin loved John Grouse . . . well, most of Berlin, and this devotion would continue for some time after the music had died.

Things began to break down immediately after the concert, though looking back at other events, all the bad things happened late at night or in the hours after the gig had finished. The niggles began as soon as the band walked into the dressing room, and I wonder how much happier I might have felt if they had never indulged in those horrible and destructive substances. Yet, perhaps a band without alcohol or drugs is an orchestra.

In order to stay on the road and keep the band's excesses flowing, we had to run the operation like a business. This meant that to save costs, the crew were expected to perform numerous duties — loading and unloading equipment, rigging up wiring and lighting, and acting as security guards for the expensive gear and unruly band members. This latter role was the most contentious, as none of us were particularly big or expert in a martial art. We had already lost poor Gibby, and the crew were well aware that at some point, situations could become awkward, even dire. And this dire part was eventually reached in Berlin.

Just like my acquaintance with Penny, I met Amelie before she had the chance to hook up with John. However, Amelie clearly had no interest in me, and her sole objective was to get an introduction. I'd dealt with similar circumstances many times before, but this situation felt different from the start. The warning lights were flashing, but I was too slow to react.

We had left the stadium and had moved on to a popular city nightclub. A small, raised area had been set aside for the band's personal use and enjoyment. I always found these situations surreal. Although the normal paying customers could see you, only our crew and a couple of borrowed bouncers had the authority to decide who could slip through the ropes and socialise with the band inside the VIP area. The power you hold is both extraordinary and uncomfortable. I remember a group of three women approaching us and one of them being turned away by a crew member because he didn't think that she was attractive enough. Perhaps far worse, was the fact that her two friends didn't hesitate to join us. I could only assume that the sight of John, bare-chested Ochie, and the extortionate display of booze awaiting consumption had completely soured their minds. Then, Amelie arrived.

The first thing that struck me as slightly unusual, was that the club owners were very insistent that her small party should have access to the band. No questions asked. Secondly, it was strange that the club bouncers had temporarily deserted their posts. There were five in Amelie's party, a peculiar group made up of three large ugly men, and two exceptionally beautiful women. I can still recall what Amelie was wearing that night — a pleated chequered mini skirt, a silk blouse, and long white boots. She had blonde hair and green feline eyes. I can remember these details clearly, because two hours later I would be compelled to get very close to Amelie. Far too close.

It wasn't my job to upset our club hosts, so I personally led the group to the drinks table and invited them to help themselves. Two of the men were eager to indulge and immediately got stuck into a bottle of vodka. It's a worn and widely used description, but their crude mannerisms did remind me of pigs at a trough. They had tight cropped hair, black trousers, and ill-fitting jackets, a sort of unfunny version of *Laurel and Hardy*. I had no idea what nationality they were or how they earned a living. I think at that moment in time, I wanted to believe that they were harmless off-duty chauffeurs who had driven a larger party to the gig and then abandoned their Mercedes cars outside the club. I'd seen stranger things over the years. Perhaps the serious-looking man — who wasn't drinking alcohol — was going to drive them home. But Amelie was less interested in our generous free alcohol. 'You take me to John, yes?' she said persuasively.

My usual reaction would have been one of caution. I would have liked to have asked her a few preliminary questions to ensure that she wasn't a lunatic with a knife in her handbag. But the club owners seemed to know quite a lot about her, and John would not be disappointed. Of course, he wasn't. After a brief introduction, he quickly abandoned an oriental girl with a green wig and bright orange lips, and I was despatched to the drinks table to collect two crystal glasses and a large bottle of tequila. Once I had completed this task, I returned to my duties and did not think about Amelie; until Karl, our longsuffering tour manager, grabbed me firmly by the arm. It was now quarter to two in the morning.

'We have to get back to the hotel,' he said agitatedly.

'Why?' I asked. 'What's happened?'

'Just bloody well come with me, okay?' It was rare that Karl lost his temper, although he was prone to the odd moment of stress. No one could remain entirely calm when you worked for *The Grouse*.

There was a taxi waiting for us in the street, and we were joined by another crew member, Bradley, who looked equally confused.

'They've bloody well found out where John is staying,' Karl said angrily, 'they probably bribed one of the club staff, but I hope it's got fuck all to do with one of our crew.'

'Who has found out?' I asked.

'Those three bloody goons that barged their way into our private party. John has left the club with a blonde woman who just happens to be the bloody girlfriend of some local gangster. A real nasty piece of work.'

'Hold on! John left the club on his own?' Bradley said with alarm.

'John does what the fuck he likes. Where have you been for the last six months?'

'But we didn't see him leave.'

'Maybe you weren't looking out for a rock star wearing a green wig and a fur coat. But that's what I'm hearing from spaced-out Ochie.'

'And who else did Ochie talk to?' Bradley said.

We all knew what he was thinking.

'This girl was definitely blonde and not oriental?' I asked.

'Yes. Blonde, mini skirt, white boots. Fucking gorgeous. *Why?*'

'Because it might have been the blonde who borrowed the wig for John and then arranged the getaway,' I said, my voice tight with the guilt of knowing that I was the one who had introduced her to John. 'She had an agenda and then saw an opportunity to get to him. And it sounds like she would also have to give her minders the slip. But where's the gangster boyfriend?'

'Out of town. These goons must be the second-rate heavies, which makes them even more desperate to get back their charge. It's a tricky situation and the club owners are shitting themselves. *We're really sorry to tell you, but right under our noses, some English rock star shagged your bird last night.* I wouldn't be surprised if this gangster has a stake in the business.'

When we arrived at the hotel, Karl threw a wad of cash at the taxi driver and asked him to stay where he was. But I doubted that the German driver understood the instruction. We dashed inside the lobby and saw the three heavies leaning over the reception desk. 'Craig, get up to John's room and get that bloody woman the hell out of there,' Karl said. 'You're the only one he'll open the door to. We'll try to do something down here — but fuck knows what!'

I ignored the lift and ran up six flights of stairs to reach the third floor. I didn't stop until I reached John's room. It took three large bangs with my fist before the door opened. John was swaying precariously in front of me wearing just a Grouse T-shirt and the green wig. Behind him, I could see the woman lying face down on the bed. She was naked. 'Christ!' I panted. 'What have you done to her?'

'Are you kidding,' his words slurred. 'No chance of any action with this one. Look at the state she's in!'

'I meant, is she breathing?'

'Groaning, gurgling, you name it. She can't take the pace,' he said bitterly. 'You got another girl for me?'

'No! For fuck's sake, John. This is a gangster's moll and her minders are very keen to collect her.'

'Thank God for that. They're very welcome to her.'

'Jesus! They're after blood. *Your blood!* This is serious. We need to get her out of your room and quickly.'

'Right! Fuck! She's hardly dressed for a taxi ride.'

'Yeah,' I said frustratedly, 'so we're going to have to dress her.'

I remember the next few minutes as being something akin to a *Benny Hill* sketch, although only John managed to find comedy moments in our ridiculous and frantic attempts to dress the poor woman. 'It's much easier the other way,' he commented, whilst trying to reattach her bra. We completely botched pulling up her underwear, as the little lace ribbons seemed to be on the wrong side. I was relieved that she wasn't wearing tights or stockings. Fortunately, the pleated skirt covered this minor panty discrepancy, and the coarse woollen fabric was much easier to manoeuvre. Finally, I lifted her shoulders and John tugged the silk blouse over her arms. Thankfully, her breasts were pert, and it felt like dressing a Barbie doll. Then, I dragged her unceremoniously out of the room and propped her crudely against the corridor wall. She'd remained comatose the whole time. 'What a waste,' John muttered, as he tossed out her white boots. 'The girl had potential.'

I stacked the boots neatly by her side and told John to go back into his room. 'Lock and bolt the door,' I warned him. 'And don't open it until the morning.'

I had concocted some sort of a plan whilst we had been awkwardly dressing Amelie. It wasn't ideal. I decided to go back down to the reception point and raise the alarm. I'd say that I heard an inebriated girl banging on doors and wandering aimlessly around the third-floor corridor. Her ugly companions could then go and collect her. Unfortunately, the elevator door opened before I had managed even a few steps from where Amelie was so crudely slumped. The three heavies blustered into the corridor and then rushed menacingly towards me. 'I might have known.' He was the serious-looking man who had declined our generous offer of alcohol. 'It's that shitty security guy from the club. What the fuck have you done to her?'

'I'm sorry?'

'*What have you fucking done to her?*'

'I'm not aware that anyone has dared to go near her,' I said with as much composure as I could muster. 'Ten minutes ago, she was banging on every door along this corridor like a lunatic. Do you know which is her room?'

'Idiot!' he shouted. 'You fucking idiot! Why did you bring her here?'

'I didn't,' my voice quivered. 'I've only just arrived from the night club.'

'*What?* Then you're a liar! You just said ten minutes ago she was . . .'

'And when did you leave?' I interrupted him.

To my alarm, the other two heavies were standing outside John's door now. I realised that the receptionist must have given something away, and for some reason, Karl and Bradley had been unable to stall them. One of the heavies was sinisterly tracing his finger over the door number, whilst carefully twisting the handle with his other hand. None of them seemed to care about Amelie.

'There's a bloke asleep in that room with his pregnant wife,' I protested.

'You dead, Grouse!' the man shouted in broken English. 'Fucking dead!'

'Why don't you help the young lady.' My voice was barely audible now.

'Excuse me?' The non-drinker said aggressively, before moving within a few inches of my face. 'Listen to me, you idiot little man. So loyal to this great fucking rock 'n' roll legend, huh? Well, you're a fucking idiot. And why? Because you have no idea the trouble you are in, *understand?*'

The door that led to the stairs was slowly swinging open. Two heads emerged. Karl and Bradley peered sheepishly down the corridor. Like a weight being lifted off my shoulders, I sensed the pressure easing slightly. *Three against three.* 'But I do understand,' I said, desperately trying to control the tension in my voice, 'you see, if things get violent here, then the press will be all over it and questions will be asked about why this poor young lady was in John Grouse's hotel. But none of us want this fact to be known, do we? Just take the poor girl away, and everything will be fine.'

He lifted his huge forearm and slowly dragged his fingers across his nose. *'Everything will be fine,'* he childishly mimicked my voice. 'I'm going to hit you so fucking hard.'

'But why won't it be fine? It's not as if anything has happened. She's just had too much to drink. Nothing that a long sleep won't cure.'

'Long sleep? Simple, *yeah?*' He glowered at me. 'Simple for who?'

'Simple for all of us. You take her away, and there isn't going to be a problem. No one will know that she was here.'

'Okay,' he thought for a moment, before jabbing his finger towards me. 'We do this one thing. But I tell you, the press won't give a shit when we break your bones in the morning. *Because you are fucking nobody.* Nothing. So get the fuck out of Berlin, idiot little man.' He turned and said something to his companions. They scowled at him, and a small argument broke out. Then he raised his voice and gestured angrily towards Amelie. Reluctantly, the two of them picked her up and carried her towards the elevator. He turned to address me again, and to my surprise, he began to laugh. 'You know why I don't hit you? Yes?'

I shrugged.

'Because I pity you,' he continued. 'Look at you. The pathetic little man who will never get the girl. That's right, isn't it? And how does that feel?' He shook his head and followed the others down the corridor. 'Oh yes, I know. It feels like shit. Get the fuck out of Berlin!'

I stood in a daze, my hands vibrating against my face.

'You don't need to worry about those threats,' Karl said genially after the heavies had disappeared, 'you won't see them again.'

'I know,' I said bitterly. 'Why would they be interested in a pathetic, little bloke like me.'

'Don't be hard on yourself. You played it well, they certainly won't want their boss to know that she came here.'

'Played it well? Is that what you used to tell Gibby?' I asked him. 'And what about the next jealous or psychotic boyfriend who comes looking for John? Am I meant to play the stupid superhero every night? No, I've had enough of this. I've had enough of the rotten atmosphere in the band, the malice and fighting. I'm packing right now and heading for the airport.'

'You can't! What about driving the fucking coach?'

'Hire someone. I'm not like Ochie, drivers are two a penny. I quit.'

'Okay, you're right.' He sighed. 'Take a break from the tour, have a few days to get your head straight, even a week — you deserve it. But then get in touch with me. You owe it to John.'

'I'm sorry?' I shoved my elbow hard into the wall. 'I owe it to John! Do I really? *For fuck's sake.* Don't you get it? That's the problem — right there. It's always been the problem.'

'Craig, listen to me. John needs you.'

'No. That's just it. John needs me to be like some kind of doting and supportive big brother. From the first day we met, it's always been that way. I'm sorry, but I can't do this anymore.'

I never did get in touch with Karl, because that was the night that I turned my back on *The Grouse Conspiracy*.

***

It was awkward saying goodbye to Grace, Frank and Sean. I felt that it was a question of protocol — who should stand up first, and, whether the polite thing to do was to leave the bar at the same time. It reminded me of the breaking up process and the end of my romantic relationships. I'd certainly had quite a bit of practice. But I never understood men who couldn't let go of a relationship. If one party is unhappy, then why draw out the discomfort? It's like being ten minutes into a bad film and knowing that there's another two hours left to endure.

The breakup with Penny was the simplest. She disappeared one day. There was no warning or drama, and no evidence that she had even existed. Just another empty property seeking a new tenant. I made no attempt to look for her, besides, there was no road, no bridleway to follow.

*Would my relationship with Juliet last?* I had no idea. It wasn't something that I felt I needed to dwell on. I had learnt that there was life after *The Grouse*, and our strange blue planet offered other opportunities. I had always found that the easy option was to walk away. To move on. Another venue, another city. Like a rock band on tour.

It was Grace who stood up first, and her devoted family obediently copied her. I got the impression that Grace ruled the family home, and she could be feisty if she needed to be. "It's been such a lovely day," she said warmly, "and I hope you enjoy the rest of your holiday." Then, gently patting Olivia's arm. "Oh, and my regards and best wishes to your mother."

The men just smiled and took it in turns to shake my hand. Sean gave Olivia a little hug and moved after his mother, but Frank shuffled his feet uneasily, his shoulders rocking as he adjusted his weight. He hesitated, then leant his head towards me, clumsily pushing his mouth against my ear. "In case you were wondering," he whispered, "my brother came with me to see *The Grouse* on that night in Belfast." His breathing was now heavy and laboured. "It was how I managed to identify his body . . . I mean, from the shreds of torn cloth. You see, he was wearing it . . . Wearing the band's T-shirt on the day that he died."

I simply nodded my head. There were no words that I could offer, no more stories to tell. Just like John and the band, Korčula's Old Town walls guarded a rich and extraordinary script that was way beyond anything I could understand. So, Olivia and I sat in silence watching the family stroll away, waiting for their silhouettes to be swallowed by the backdrop of the sea.

"Do you want another drink?" I asked her. "It doesn't have to be a cocktail. Perhaps a latte or a soft drink?"

She smiled. "You know, I'd really like a cup of tea."

"That's a good choice."

The waiter didn't need any persuasion to return to our table. After taking our order, he took his time to clear the glasses and then made a feeble joke about his heavy load. Olivia appeared to be a little distracted by him or maybe her thoughts were elsewhere. "I wish I had some musical ability," she said reticently. "My mother can play the piano, but I'm useless — just like Daddy."

"I'm the same," I said. "When I was at school, my mother wanted me to sing in the school choir. The grumpy music teacher was desperate for new recruits. But no, my voice wasn't good enough, so I still got rejected! Then she made me take violin lessons, but again, I was absolutely useless."

Olivia screwed up her nose and scowled at me. "But what about when you were with the band?"

"I wasn't paid to go anywhere near the stage. I was the driver of the tour bus, because the band couldn't manoeuvre a mini out of a supermarket car park. We all have our roles in life. It's like a jigsaw. A whole bunch of tiny pieces that are pinned together to help form something recognisable."

She sighed. "What's my role then? Daddy says I'm rubbish at schoolwork. He wasn't happy with my exam results."

"Well, John Grouse apparently died in tragic circumstances whilst trying to take a photograph. But if you'd been around at the time, the band would have some amazing pictures of them performing on stage. And I've got nothing to help me remember the places we visited."

"That's a lie. You've never seen my photographs."

"Yes, but I've spent most of my life around great and unusual talent. I can sense it. Forget the driving, maybe that's my true purpose in this strange and crazy world — sensing talent."

"Your purpose?" she said sceptically.

"And why not? It will be my obituary."

"That's a funny thing to write on a gravestone."

"Fair enough. But perhaps during breakfast tomorrow

morning, you could show me the photographs?"

"Maybe." Her gaze slipped into her lap, and she stubbornly kept the same posture, even when the waiter brought our hot drinks. There were times like this when I didn't understand women.

I waited for the young man to leave before speaking again. "You want to know a secret?"

She shrugged.

"I was rubbish at school, too. That's why I drive a silly lorry."

"Great! So now you think I should drive a lorry!"

I laughed. "No, not necessarily. I think you should find your own way. And when you do, you'll be great at it."

"Being rubbish at things might not just be down to me," she said defiantly. "Maybe if I had a father who used to be a hellraising rock 'n' roll roadie, things might be better. How am I meant to do well at school when people are cruel to me because they think Daddy is an arrogant bastard? Is it my fault no one seems to like him?"

Her outburst and anger towards her father threw me. Although, I felt genuine sympathy for her rather than any satisfaction. "No, of course that's not your fault. But remember, a lot of people are misjudged. I wasn't really a hellraising roadie. I was the one who had to stay sober and drive the bus in the morning. Perceptions can be wrong."

"*Really?* Have you met Daddy's stupid girlfriend? She's all face packs, designer dresses, and put-downs. No wonder people don't like us. Oh, and she's far too busy slagging off the neighbours to find a job."

I picked up my drink and watched the clouds sketching patterns along the ridge of the mountain. "She's not your mother, Olivia. You don't have to like her." I hesitated, taking a sip of my latte. "You don't have to like me either."

"I don't!" She laughed, her fingers tenderly cupping her chin. "I'm kidding! My God, your fight with Desmond the deer was hilarious. And then you so bravely took on those ants! I'd love to see Daddy's stupid girlfriend get attacked by vicious ants."

The sunlight wavered, and I watched the shadows of the Old

Town creep across the table. "Well," I said deviously, "you could always sneak a few inside her designer frocks."

\*\*\*

'Do you remember Moonlight and Vodka?'

I can still recall the sound of John's voice. We were sitting in a restaurant overlooking the stunning Ponte Vecchio in Florence.

I had smiled and briefly gazed across the river Arno. *'Fix me a drink, make it a strong one. Hey comrade, a drink, make it a long one!'* Then, acknowledging the song's lyrics, I had raised my wine glass to him. 'Chris De Burgh's concert in Manchester.'

'Absolutely, my friend. The moment that defined our lives.'

'You mean because it was the night that we first met?'

'Good point, and equally important.' He appeared to be distracted by a piece of fish and began to chase it stubbornly around his plate. 'But no, not that. I was referring to the tiny figure standing on the stage inside that huge arena. Except, through my eyes, it wasn't Chris De Burgh — I was the performer looking out at the audience. Yes, I know it has happened hundreds of times since, yet on that night, I swear I could see the faces of the fans staring back at me. That was the moment that I knew.' He leaned back in his chair, looked directly into my eyes and majestically sang the final verse of the song. *'Moonlight and vodka, takes me away, midnight in Moscow is sunshine in LA.'*

Yet far beneath us, and whispered softly within the aloof and chilly patterns of the river, I could hear other lyrics from the song. *'My hands are shaking, and my feet are numb, my head is aching and the bar's going round, and I'm so down, in this foreign town.'*

# CHAPTER FOURTEEN

Five years have passed since that beautiful day in Korčula. I will never forget it, and Olivia is so keen to share those wonderful memories with me.

She is in her early twenties now and lives in London. But when she visits the village, she will always pop into the Social Club to seek me out. It's a pleasure to break off from my pint to have a chat with her. I've even been known to abandon a game of snooker to have a catch-up. I've no idea what it means, but she still calls me 'Cowboy'. I suspect she does it because it always makes me smile.

To my surprise — because not for a single moment did I ever expect it to happen — Olivia earns a living working as a photographer. Of course, I have never admitted this to her. Perhaps encouraging talent really is my 'purpose' in life. She mainly does weddings or family occasions, but she's sold a few of her own photographs as well. She has some incredible pictures of the London skyline on her website. Yes, she is extremely fortunate that her father's money helps to cover some of the bills and the overheads, but her reputation is beginning to grow. 'One day I'll be able to pay him back in full,' she told me firmly. I have a good feeling that she will.

My breakup with her mother hit Olivia hard. She described it as going through a second divorce following her parents' split, and I fully understand what she meant. I still remember my father leaving home, the uncertainty and the desolation. It was Juliet's decision to break up, and at least I was able to demonstrate to Olivia that a relationship can end in an amicable manner.

So, I've been on my own for three years now. I believe that I'm happy. I have a white van rather than a lorry, and local deliveries are popular. Divorced ladies still need help to transport pieces of furniture to their new lodgings. But I'm not sure that you can find love in your early sixties.

Juliet thinks that she has found love. Unsurprisingly, Olivia doesn't get along with the new boyfriend. I cheekily suggested that they should all go on holiday to Korčula, although I would be devastated if this were to happen.

Six months ago, I heard that Ochie had died of a heart attack. He had been living in Hanoi, Vietnam. I was in my van listening to the radio when the announcement was made. It was a Wednesday afternoon. Two hours later, I put on my hiking boots and set off for the bleak moorland that surrounds the village. It was a crisp and sunny day in March, and I walked a round trip of about six miles. Then, as dusk fell, I called in at the Social Club and drank a beer and a couple of whiskeys. I finally made my peace with *The Grouse Conspiracy*.

*The End*

# SOME INTRIGUING QUESTIONS

*\* Where is Korčula?*

Korčula is an island that is just off the Croatian mainland and Dalmatian coast. It is equidistant from two cities, Split and Dubrovnik. The trip across from the mainland takes approximately fifteen minutes by boat; the Pelješac Channel being just 1.2 kilometres wide. The island is considered to be the birthplace of Marco Polo, which is evident when you walk through Korčula's Old Town — a medieval walled city that strides magnificently into the Pelješac Channel.

*\* Why did you set the story on Korčula?*

Some places become very special to us, and a bit like love, their beauty and wonderment can bowl you over. You could even argue that they have a spiritual effect on the soul. After visiting such places, some of us gaze longingly at our holiday photographs, others feel compelled to write reviews or travel blogs, and I wrote this book — *sorry about that!* The experience of writing felt like an extended holiday. Usually, I have a story already in place in my head, and when I find the right place, I put the two together. With Korčula, I just had the place. Fortunately, the outline of the plot came to me before I arrived back home in England, but it was a long flight! I knew from the first chapter that the narrator (Craig) drove a lorry, was drawn to divorcees, and had a prickly relationship with Juliet's daughter (Olivia). But I was quite deep into the book before John Grouse suddenly appeared in my subconscious. Then, just like his memory haunted Craig, he began to monopolise the story and stamp his presence on the book. *The Grouse Conspiracy* was born.

*\* Have you visited Dubrovnik?*

Yes, I have. I've walked the streets that were cruelly bombed during the Siege of Dubrovnik (October 1991 to May 1992) and visited the Museum of Croatian War of Independence which is housed in the Napoleonic Fort Imperial close to the cable car station on Mount Srđ. The character of Ana is very real, because after such a painful conflict, it is sometimes human nature to leave a country that you once cherished so dearly.

*\* Have you ever visited Belfast?*

Yes, but I have kept my response to the end of this Q&A, as my recollections are quite detailed.

*\* Is the snorkelling and wine tour based on fact?*

Absolutely. All the places are real. Boats and organised excursions leave Korčula Old Town daily during the tourist season. Alternatively, you can use the hop-on-hop-off water taxis to reach the surrounding islands.

My special thanks go to *Korčula Explorer.*

*\* Frank was obsessed with shady stories about the band. Did you find it difficult to create such sleazy rock and roll tales?*

Ashamedly, I didn't! This part of the book felt like a sequel to one of my first stories: *Hassle Castle.* Many of *The Grouse's* indulgencies are based on events that I have witnessed. But I'll stop there.

*\* Do you have any musical ability?*

None. I'm just like Craig, hence, I didn't even attempt to throw octaves or chords into any of the dialogue or paragraphs. My belief is that you should write about what you know. Yes, I have had to research some basic facts about Korčula, but you need to taste the air of a place to be able to describe what a character is seeing and feeling. As I don't understand how to create music, John Grouse could never have been my narrator.

*\* Is John Grouse based on anyone famous?*

No, because I don't know anyone famous. He is an amalgamation of two separate people. But I've certainly watched budding musicians perform in empty bars or at talent nights. After having written so many books myself, I have felt both their creative ecstasy and frustration.

*\* The book cover*

Unfortunately for Mario, the boat on the cover is not his. The picture is based on a photograph taken by Sabine (cover creator and editor) and was designed solely for the purpose of the story. I think it beautifully depicts Korčula and the splendid vessels that visit her. This is the view that Grace, Frank and Sean would have seen as they strolled into the Old Town. *Frank's Bar* is tucked away out of sight on the right of the painting.

*\* Chris De Burgh*

Yes, I found him in Manchester, then in Liverpool. Thank you for your wonderful songs and storytelling.

*\* About my visit to Belfast?*

These are my recollections of my only visit to the city nearly forty years ago. At this point in my life, I was a twenty-year old student living in Lancashire, England, and had little understanding of what it meant to live in Northern Ireland or why so many people were tragically losing their lives since the start of the conflict in the late 1960s.

On Wednesday, 2nd November 1983, I climbed onto a fifty-seater coach outside Preston Polytechnic, and we set off towards the South West of Scotland. We were a motley crew of aspirational rugby players, hockey players, badminton specialists etc. and my two fellow male squash players. Our destination was the Ulster Polytechnic in Belfast (it changed to University of Ulster in 1984), and we needed to catch the late afternoon ferry from Stranraer.

Competitive sport with other colleges was quite limited, and Ulster and Liverpool Polytechnic were part of the triangle of colleges that we played against. Home and away fixtures alternated each year.

*Were we scared about travelling to Belfast?* No, but we were certainly apprehensive. On a daily basis, the television news reminded us of *The Troubles* in Northern Ireland, and additionally, there had been recent devastating bomb attacks in London, Birmingham, and Bristol. Yet, being typical students, the ferry crossing was a babble of raucous excitement, intermingled with periods of manic singing and heavy drinking.

It was dark when we arrived in Belfast, and our lovely student hosts were waiting to greet us on the quay. After some hurried introductions, we were told that we would be transported to the Polytechnic in two minibuses, and that due to our large numbers, a couple of trips would be required. Squash players are generally decent chaps, and along with a few of the rugby players, we offered to wait for the minibuses to return.

This decision would turn out to be quite dramatic.

Firstly, because a couple of the rugby players decided that they would take the opportunity to visit a nearby pub for a swift pint of Guinness. Unfortunately, there was a metal fence blocking their route, and after clumsily climbing to the top, one of them managed to slip and spear his leg on a sharp metal stake. He didn't make the pub or the minibus, and he had to leave the quay in an ambulance. Secondly, when the minibus returned to collect us, the chilled driver had more time on his hands. He casually remarked: "There's no rush now as you lot are the last to be picked up, so how about we take a trip down the Falls Road? It's always a popular request from tourists!"

This statement was met with genuine gasps of horror. The Falls Road — meaning 'territory of the enclosures' — is the main road through west Belfast, but due to its republican roots (Irish republicans view British rule of any part of Ireland as inherently illegitimate), it was synonymous with brutal murders and kidnappings. Not an area that you would find recommended in a 1980s tourist map. Besides, hadn't we just seen enough blood shed for one evening? But the student driver shrugged off our concerns. "I grew up there, but just as a precaution, I promise I'll keep the doors locked!"

My memories of this fairly short excursion were of my desperate efforts to resurrect my Welsh accent, so if required, I could demonstrate my neutral nationality (I had lived the first ten years of my life in South Wales — which was half my damned life!). I also remember the strange normality of this long city road that was hauntingly lit up beneath the cold November sky (sometimes it is reputation and not the physical landscape that define places), and the beautiful, yet, intimidating political murals that were painted on the end of the rows of terraced housing. But like a rollercoaster ride, it was quickly over, and we gratefully arrived at our destination.

After our hosts had shown us where we would be sleeping — a grubby rubber gymnastics mat in the middle of a cold sports hall — we were invited to attend a disco in the Student Union bar. As I carefully placed my sleeping bag on the sticky rubber surface, it dawned on me that I had been allocated a tiny space amongst my fellow male Preston students, including the drunk and rowdy rugby team. It would undoubtedly be a long and difficult night with zero privacy. Beer was the only solution. Preferably, lots of it.

It was an excellent disco, although, as a budding storyteller, my most vivid recollection of the event was the disturbing and eerie graffiti on the toilet walls. *God Save Our Queen*, on one side, and something akin to *Murder the Bloody English Scum*, on the opposite wall. It felt like being in the middle of a violent — yet silent — argument, which is quite unsettling when you have your pants around your ankles, and you're in a strange and confusing environment.

The reality of the sleeping arrangements was far worse than I could have imagined — a filthy waft of body odour, unruly intestines, gorilla-like belching, and loud snoring. Time seemed to crawl across the dusty floor like a one-legged sloth. It felt like I was violently awoken every fifteen minutes, and by quarter past six in the morning I had made up my mind to pack up my kit and flee. I never wanted to set eyes on that bleak gymnasium ever again. Unsurprisingly, I was closely followed by another member of our squash team, Ibrar. Once again, this decision would leave a lasting impression on me.

The campus sits on the shore of Belfast Lough, an inlet of the Irish Sea, and after taking a long shower, we were both keen to get some fresh air. Slipping out of the fire exit, we were delighted to be greeted by a magnificent sunrise. However, our escape was quickly interrupted by the hostile challenge of two clearly jittery security guards. Our surprise and confusion were evident to the guards, as the only security presence we had encountered in Preston, were the slow and hefty bouncers at the Friday Night Disco. And never this early in the day. Fortunately, once the purpose of our visit to Belfast had been explained, they were happy for us to carry on with our stroll.

We were still quite shaken when we reached the magnificent and idyllic shoreline, and I distinctly remember saying to Ibrar: "As a Muslim, you must be feeling like one of the safest people in this crazy city."

Ibrar responded in his usual cutting manner. "No, I don't feel at all safe. But if anything does kick off, you're on your own, Mate!"

Unsurprisingly, we didn't win our squash match. The late disco and sleep deprivation didn't help our cause, but they were an exceptionally strong team.

We left Belfast in the early afternoon, and due to our collective fatigue, the homeward journey was far more subdued. Even the few winners amongst us appeared to be too tired to celebrate or gloat. But the winning or losing is immaterial, and this narrative is nothing without the tragic and shocking event that happened on the following Friday morning. This is the reason why I have felt compelled to put these memories onto this page.

Having been excused from Friday lectures and seminars, I had woken late, and it was lunchtime before I headed to my familiar surroundings in the Preston Student Union. I was in the queue for a chip buttie, when one of the badminton players told me to pop next door to the television lounge and watch the national news. Arriving at the small, seating area behind the pool tables, the pictures of Belfast Lough seemed very familiar to me, and these are the cold grey words that resonated:

*Belfast, Northern Ireland. A bomb believed to be planted by Irish nationalist guerrillas exploded today in a college classroom. Two police officers were killed and about thirty other people were injured. Police said one officer was killed instantly, and the second, a sergeant, died of his injuries several hours later from the blast at Ulster Polytechnic. Police sources said they feared at last two other victims would die.*

More than 3,500 people were killed in the conflict, which stretched from the late 1960s until the Good Friday Agreement of 1998 (the date often deemed to be the end of *The Troubles*). There is a striking, poignant, and beautiful film (released in 2019) and a book by the same name, which portrays some of the personal stories during this extremely sad period. It's called: *Lost Lives*.

Thank you for reading *The Grouse Conspiracy* (or for just finding this page). If you have enjoyed the story and believe others may also be interested in this reading experience, you are very welcome to submit a review or share your thoughts on social forums (e.g. Goodreads). Likewise, please visit my website at:

www.martynchapmanauthor.co.uk

# ONE CHRISTMAS IN NUREMBERG

## By Martyn Chapman

Forced to confront the sorrows of her past, Daniela invites Simon to accompany her to the historical city of Nuremberg and its enchanting Christmas Market. But Simon is also burdened by memories of a hidden tragedy, and, drawn in by his bachelor lifestyle; he has a cynical view of the festive period.

Together, they explore Nuremberg's bewitching cobbled streets and discover that the city's poignant and cruel secrets mirror their own. As Simon is gradually charmed by the quaint wooden market stalls and glorious old buildings, he realises that Nuremberg's ghosts can help to redeem the past and unravel the truth about his own relationship with Daniela.

*One Christmas in Nuremberg* is a modern Christmas short story, played out in a traditional and magical Christmas setting.

# CHAPTER ONE

*Halloween 2015*

Perhaps it was a coincidence, but it was the night before Halloween when she had received that extraordinary message.

Through my eyes, it would simply have looked like a muddle of black and incoherent letters, although those few German words would shortly transform everything that I had always believed about humanity, friendship, and enchantingly, the very meaning of Christmas.

As soon as I settled down opposite her at that dishevelled canteen table, I knew that she was eager to tell me something important. "He's been in touch again," she said earnestly, "but this time it's different."

I put down my cup and plate on the coloured leaflet that advertised 'a night of ghouls, witches, and spooky tunes'. "Different?" I said, gazing warily into her pale blue eyes. "You mean it's different from stalking you?"

She smiled. "Yes, this is even more intriguing."

We always met up at lunchtime and ate our meals together. Usually, we would go down to the canteen on the ground floor of our workplace. On some occasions we would venture into the centre of Sheffield, teasing the pigeons with our sandwiches and hot sausage rolls. These engagements were not something we had ever discussed, they just felt like the right thing to do. Initially, we had almost subconsciously chosen one of the tables hidden away near the window or met up later when the majority of our colleagues had returned to their desks. Then, after a few weeks, I realised that Daniela was happy to be seen in my company and she shrugged off the whispers or the sly, derisive glances.

We were part of a large team of civil servants. When Daniela had first joined the department eighteen months ago, she had taken up residence at the desk opposite my own. But it was only when we had attended the same residential training course in London that our friendship had grown into something a little more profound.

From her very first day in the office, Daniela's svelte figure had caught the attention of many of the men on our section. However, her discreet nature and aloof personality had been less popular with some of the women.

I felt that I had a good working relationship with all the team. My position was fairly junior but I knew that I was respected for my work experience and knowledge. It was the social scene that set Daniela and me apart from the rest. The men seemed to understand why I would decline their offers to join them for a drink on a Friday evening, but Daniela's absence from the raucous city centre bars continued to frustrate them.

"I received the message yesterday evening," Daniela said, as she chased a piece of carrot with her fork. "He wants to meet me."

I picked up my coffee and frowned. "And you're not concerned about that?"

"Of course I am, Simon, but I've decided that I have to do this. It's important to me."

"Really?"

"Yes." She sullenly pointed to a message on her mobile phone, as if to suggest that this simple gesture was justification that she was doing the right thing. She knew that I couldn't understand what was written on the screen, so she nonchalantly pushed her phone to the side of the table.

"And what ridiculous hour in the morning did you make this decision?" I asked. "Half past five?"

She cast one of her delightfully alluring smiles. Her sleeping habits both amused and astonished me. "Probably earlier."

I grimaced. "So how will this meeting work? Has he suggested a venue?"

"Yes, Nuremberg."

"*What?* Excuse my ignorance, but isn't that quite a long way from your family in Munich?"

"It's about a two hour car ride. I can't find a direct flight to Nuremberg, so it would make more sense for me to catch a plane to Stuttgart. I could then complete the journey by train."

"Have you visited this city before?"

"I don't think so."

I shook my head and cut open my baked potato. "I know Germany is your home, Daniela, but you've never met this man. It could be very awkward for you."

"I agree."

"You do?"

"*Yes, Simon, I do.* So I'd like someone to come with me."

"Oh." I paused to consider her statement. "Your cousin?"

"She'd never agree to that."

"Who then?"

"Well, I do have someone in mind." She leant back in her chair and swept her blonde hair from her forehead. "Someone who will be delighted to miss our wretched Christmas party."

In spite of being seated, I felt a sudden hot and trembling sensation running down my legs. "Me?"

She nodded. "Simon, you've always shown an interest in my life."

*You've always shown an interest.* "Well ... I ..."

"And you know all my secrets."

"All of them?"

She didn't answer.

"Wow!" I said hurriedly, "I'm not sure what to say." I couldn't look at her now. My face was blushing as if the change in colour was trying to conceal some graffiti written across my cheeks. Uncomfortably, I scooped up a piece of tuna that was dribbling slowly from the top of the potato.

"You could say: 'when do we leave, Daniela?' I've checked the office diary and nearly everyone wants to be off between

Christmas and New Year, except you of course. There's typically no days requested by you at all." She quickly rocked back towards me. "Unless money is an issue?"

I felt my body begin to relax a little. "I never go anywhere to spend my vast fortune."

"I know! Nuremberg is a beautiful and historical city and it's December of course, so we can visit the Christmas Market."

I frowned. "You were doing so well."

"*Yes, I am!* And the meeting will only be for a couple of hours — perhaps even less. We'd be there for three nights and then return home on Christmas Eve." She stretched her head across the table, her voice lowered to a whisper. "Don't you see, Simon? It's perfect. You can be at the meeting to support me, but it will still be private as you won't understand a single word that's being spoken."

I mused over her statement. "But what will he think about my presence?"

"I don't care. He might think otherwise, but he doesn't know anything about my life."

# SAVING WORMS

## By Martyn Chapman

It should have been a simple story: *quirky boy meets delectable, yet mysterious girl and then boy stumbles haplessly in love*. Except this forty-two year old male has a humiliating secret and although the inevitable discovery should lead to just one of two definitive outcomes, in the befuddled world of Adam Bennett the scenarios are boundless.

*Saving Worms* is a romantic comedy that journeys from the tranquility of a Bavarian forest to the historical streets of York. And yet, ultimately, Adam's destiny will balance precariously on the whim of a Chihuahua; the intriguing Mr. Darcy; and the foreboding bedroom of the voluptuous Little Red Riding Hood.

# CHAPTER ONE

*Lenzkirch, The Black Forest,*
*Germany. September 1993*

It was late September when a hush moped across the tall pines of the forest. Autumn was approaching, and the swifts had begun to mourn the slow, dribbling demise of the hot summer months.

Eva settled down to write in front of the old stove, meticulously placing her notepad on the kitchen table. She always wrote in longhand, occasionally glancing out of the window to seek inspiration from the imperious firs that watched over the valley. Her work routine had been exactly the same for the last twenty-four years, and yet, this morning something felt very different.

Two hours earlier her beloved niece had left for the airport.

Eva was sixty-five years of age, and this would be her twelfth and final book. Pushing the top of her pencil into the disorderly folds of her chin, she tried to suppress the tiny droplets that were causing her eyes to glaze over. But inevitably, the tears began to flow.

She waited. Perhaps a few minutes had passed, before she at last began to write, her heart accepting that this story would be her most personal and her most insightful.

# BOOKS BY THIS AUTHOR

## Hassle Castle

Who is buried beneath the badger sett? And what was the heartrending fate of sweet Lorna Doom?

Lowry, the tormented and evasive narrator, is drawn back to the grounds of an empty mansion, where six letters: 'M-O-S-C-O-W' have been crudely burnt onto an old garden table. It is the abandoned scar of a tragedy that occurred three years before . . .

Thirty-four year old Dooster purchases an alluring Playboy style mansion, and his six male friends relish the elicit opportunities presented to them. The house is teasingly named Hassle Castle ('the Castle') by a disgruntled girlfriend, and to escape the creeping perils of marriage, babies, and the inevitable changes to their lives, the friends combine outrageous parties with enthralling adventures across the United Kingdom and Europe. But these humorous excursions are hooded by the men's strained loyalty to their partners, and their guarded and personal relationships with the beautiful, yet malicious Alexis, who has mysteriously disappeared. With family and police searching for her whereabouts, Lowry is haunted by Alexis's link to the Castle and disturbing memories from his childhood.

When one of the group persuades the others to accompany him to Moscow, the friends are sucked inside the menacing atmosphere of this aloof Russian city and become the victims of a devastating event. Returning home, they attempt to rebuild their shattered lives, but the dynamics of the group have fatally changed and the Castle finally reveals its dark and sinister secrets. With the past now sadistically exposed, the friends are swept towards a brutal and shocking retribution.

## Hormones And Crumble

Benjamin Rose's demise began on the day his son's tortoise committed suicide.

Ten days later he apprehensively walks into a city centre hotel, his emotions teased by the cool evening breeze on the back of his thighs and the surreal sensation of a pleated miniskirt nuzzling into the top of his stockings. Approaching the gleaming doors of the hotel elevator, he hesitates, his hand fidgeting nervously with his blonde wig, frantically summoning the courage to manoeuvre his debilitating red stilettos inside.

As the lift begins to ascend, Benjamin closes his eyes and thinks of his failing marriage, his desperation to eliminate the threats of his blackmailer, and the sinister client who is waiting for him in Room 213 . . .

## Saving Worms

It should have been a simple story: quirky boy meets delectable yet mysterious girl, and boy stumbles haplessly in love. Except, this forty-two year old boy has a humiliating secret. Although its inevitable discovery should lead to just one of two definitive outcomes, in the befuddled world of Adam Bennett the scenarios are boundless.

Saving Worms is a romantic comedy that journeys from the historical streets of York in North Yorkshire, to feisty Blackpool, and then the tranquillity of Germany's Black Forest. And yet, ultimately, Adam's destiny will balance precariously on the whim of a Chihuahua, the intriguing Mr Darcy, and the foreboding cravings of the voluptuous Little Red Riding Hood.

## The Gatehouse Haunting

After recovering from a serious illness, Ella's husband arranges for her to stay in a picturesque Gatehouse nestled within an idyllic German village. Left alone for a week to contemplate the effects of her poor health and her fractured marriage, Ella's peace is shattered by the unnerving appearance of a shadowy old woman and the chilling discovery of the graves of eleven villagers, all of whom died mysteriously on the same day. Then, strange and unsettling events begin to occur in the Gatehouse. Is someone trying to intimidate her?

## The Gulch

Will you be there for me? Will you be close by? Will you cut me down or watch me die?

Just one man applied. It was an extraordinary job interview for a unique and macabre position. Perhaps he was the only man who could meet the requirements for this delicate and very challenging role. Or, with his veiled personality and murky past, was Rod the most unsuitable?

The answer lies within a village tortured by its unspeakable history, its relentless visitors, and a burnt-out room inside an abandoned hotel.

The story is set in December. It's Christmas time. But this is far from a traditional festive tale.

## Christmas On The Law

Every Christmas Eve, a family make a short pilgrimage to

the summit of the extraordinary and mesmerising hill that dominates their small East Lothian town. They celebrate this delightful festive occasion with food, beverages, and shadowy tales of the town's historical past. But behind these seemingly innocent stories of whale bones, witchcraft, and retribution from times gone by, lies a tragic family secret that links to the present day. Will this be the Christmas Eve that the family can be reunited, and find the love and happiness that they once held so dearly?

## One Christmas In Nuremberg

Forced to confront the sorrows of her past, Daniela invites Simon to accompany her to the historical city of Nuremberg and its enchanting Christmas Market. But Simon is also burdened by memories of a hidden tragedy, and, drawn in by his bachelor lifestyle, he has a cynical view of the festive period.

Together, they explore Nuremberg's bewitching cobbled streets and discover that the city's poignant and cruel secrets mirror their own. As Simon is gradually charmed by the quaint wooden market stalls and glorious old buildings, he realises that Nuremberg's ghosts can help to redeem the past and unravel the truth about his relationship with Daniela.

One Christmas in Nuremberg is a modern Christmas short story played out in a traditional and magical Christmas setting.

## How The Boars Got Their Wild

A book for adults to share with children.

Did you know that the grumpy and wild boars that now roam Germany's enchanting Black Forest used to be happy and peaceful? It's true . . . but then a silly squirrel dropped his hazelnut in a campfire, accidentally invented cooking, stumbled upon a magical Golden Nut, and had to goof back in time to rescue his very soggy underpants . . .

Printed in Great Britain
by Amazon

27118050R00079